"How do you want to feel?"

Holly propped her chin on her hand as she thought about the question. "I don't know. I guess I was hoping for...magic."

Magic, Alex thought, remembering how his body had reacted when Holly had hugged him.

"What would magic feel like?"

She looked down at the table. "Well...goose bumps. Shivers. Your heart beating faster, your knees feeling weak. But I think I'm expecting too much."

She looked so vulnerable as she said that, her expression a little embarrassed, her cheeks turning pink. He wanted to tilt her chin up so she was looking right at him, he wanted to lean in close and—

I could make your knees feel weak, he thought.

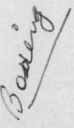

Dear Reader,

Sometimes we're our own worst enemies when it comes to love. The more self-reliant you are, the scarier falling in love can be.

It's certainly a frightening prospect for single mom Holly Stanton. She's been on her own for fifteen years, and the last thing she wants is to fall for Alex McKenna, her son's new coach and her old high school nemesis. Alex isn't ready for his feelings, either. But after spending time with the woman he once had a crush on and the boy his stepbrother abandoned, he starts to wonder if love might be worth the risk after all.

It's with great pleasure that I introduce you to Holly and Alex. They nagged me unmercifully until I put their story on paper, a story that became my first published book. I hope you have as much fun reading it as I did writing it.

My very best wishes,

Abigail

WINNING THE RIGHT BROTHER

ABIGAIL STROM

♥ *Silhouette*®

SPECIAL EDITION®

Published by Silhouette Books

America's Publisher of Contemporary Romance

SILHOUETTE BOOKS

ISBN-13: 978-0-373-65528-1

WINNING THE RIGHT BROTHER

Printed in U.S.A.

Books by Abigail Strom

Silhouette Special Edition

Winning the Right Brother #2046

ABIGAIL STROM

started writing stories at the age of seven and has never been able to stop. She's thrilled to be publishing her first book with Silhouette Special Edition, a line she has loved for many years. She works full-time as a human resources professional and lives in New England with her family, who are incredibly supportive of the hours she spends hunched over her computer.

For Tara Gorvine, who made me do it.

And for Susan Litman,
who made a dream come true with one phone call.

Chapter One

"Mom! Hey, Mom!"

"Up here, Will," Holly Stanton called out. Her son came up the stairs two at a time and stood in the doorway, tossing a football from hand to hand while she finished maneuvering her new mattress onto the box spring. She'd just spent a breathless ten minutes getting it in the house and up to her bedroom.

"Geez, Mom. Why didn't you wait till I got home? I could've helped you."

Holly grinned at her fifteen-year-old son. His auburn hair and green eyes were so like hers, but he was ten inches taller and a hundred pounds heavier.

"I didn't need any help, Squirt. I got it up here, didn't I? Hardly broke a sweat."

Will shook his head, but he was grinning back at her.

"Someone I know says you were always like this. Never letting anybody help you. Stubborn as a mule."

Holly flipped one end of a freshly laundered sheet in his direction. "Here, if you're so eager to be useful. And who's this anonymous source of yours? Weston is my hometown, you know. I thought I knew who all my old friends and enemies were."

Will tucked the bottom corner of the fitted sheet under the mattress. "Believe it or not, it's our new coach. He actually *knows* you, Mom. He remembers you from high school."

Holly looked skeptical. "The guy you've been talking about nonstop for the last two weeks? How is it that you haven't mentioned this little fact before?"

"Because I only found out today," he said as he helped his mom lay out the top sheet and smooth out the wrinkles.

"All right, what's his name? All you ever call him is Coach."

"His name is Alex. Alex McKenna."

Holly froze. She'd been stuffing one of her bed pillows into a case, and now she stood perfectly still, clutching the pillow to her chest like a security blanket.

"Alex…McKenna?"

Will nodded. "Yeah. Do you remember him? I don't think he meant to say anything about knowing you. He kind of let it slip when I was talking about you today after practice, about how you won't let me get a job to help out with bills or anything, and how you made me choose between football and basketball, because you wanted me to spend at least part of the year thinking about classes—"

"I know, I'm just crazy like that," Holly said, but her

mind was far away. Of all the memories she didn't want to revisit…

"Well, anyhow, that's when he said you'd always been stubborn. I asked how he knew you, and he said you'd gone to high school together, and you never let anyone help you back then, either. Then he kind of brushed it off and we went back to talking about football. Do you remember him?"

"Yes," Holly said.

Alex McKenna. Out of all the people she would have been happy never to hear from again, he was right at the top of the list. "I haven't seen him since we graduated. He went to college on a football scholarship, and played professionally after that. I know he quit the NFL to go into coaching, but that was the last I heard of him." She took a deep breath, looking across the bed at her son. Odds were he'd find out the rest one of these days. Better he hear it from her. "He's…related to your father."

"My father?"

Holly winced at the eagerness in his voice. "Yes. They're stepbrothers. They're not close," she warned him. "They haven't talked in years. So don't think this is a way to—"

"Connect to my dad?"

Holly felt a stab of pain at the resigned expression that replaced the eagerness in her son's green eyes. It made him seem much older than his fifteen years.

"Don't worry, Mom. I know better. And, anyway, I wouldn't say anything to Coach about it. I don't want people to think I'm trying to be a teacher's pet or something." Suddenly he was smiling again, the easy, open smile Holly knew so well. "I plan to earn my place on the team without any special favors."

"Of course you will," Holly said firmly.

Will rolled his eyes as he stuffed a pillow into a case and set it against the headboard. "Don't pretend you care, Mom. You know you hate football."

"True," Holly admitted as she plumped her pillow and reached for the blue-and-white comforter. "I do hate football—but I love you."

"Which is why you'll let me go out after dinner, right? If I promise to be back by nine?"

"On a school night?" Holly said suspiciously as the two of them spread the comforter over the bed. "To do what, exactly?"

"Oh, the usual teenage stuff. Drink some beer, do some drugs, die in a spectacular car accident they'll take pictures of for next year's driver's ed class—"

"Just keep talking, kid. Making jokes about your tragic death is definitely the way to talk me into your little excursion. Which you still haven't explained, by the way."

"It's Coach's idea. Tomorrow's the first game of the season, which you probably forgot all about, and he wants me and the other quarterbacks to come by his house for an hour or two to go over the playbook. Make sure we're all on the same page."

Holly sighed. "Homework?"

"Done."

"Transportation?"

"Coach will pick us up around seven and drop us off no later than nine, like I said."

Holly's heart skipped a beat. "Here? Alex is coming here?"

"Yes. If it's all right with the most understanding mom in the whole entire—"

Holly threw up her hands in surrender. "Fine, yes,

you can go. All I ask is that you set the table for dinner and take the lasagna out of the oven in ten minutes."

She was rewarded with a huge smile.

"Deal!" Will said.

"And don't forget to take out the trash!" Holly called after him as he headed out the door.

"No problem!" Will called back over his shoulder. He pounded down the stairs and into the kitchen, singing the Weston Wildcat fight song at the top of his lungs.

Upstairs it was suddenly quiet. For a minute Holly just stood in the middle of her room, staring at nothing. Then she moved over to the dresser and studied her reflection in the mirror that hung above it.

She hadn't seen Alex for years...not since high school, when she'd dated his stepbrother, Brian. Will's father. Brian the golden boy, with his good grades and good looks and bright future.

Then there was Alex: a year younger and everything Brian wasn't. A natural athlete and a star on the football team but wild, rebellious, always in trouble with his teachers and his coaches for mouthing off, breaking rules, flouting authority.

He'd sported a punk look back then: his hair bleached and spiked, his clothes always black—black jeans, black jacket, black combat boots. He'd played guitar and sung in a garage band, she remembered.

Where Brian was safety, Alex was danger. Where Brian was predictable, Alex was volatile. In the simple world of high school where there were good girls and bad girls, the former dreamed about Brian and the latter dreamed about Alex.

Although Holly's status as a good girl was universally acknowledged, one of her best friends was Brenda, a self-proclaimed bad girl who would talk about Alex by the hour.

"Holly, he's sex on wheels. Those arms—that *butt*—how can you not *notice?*"

Holly would blush at Brenda's graphic language and shrug her shoulders. "Not my type, I guess. And, anyway, I'm dating his—"

"Stepbrother, yeah, I know. Brian the Boring. I will definitely be your bridesmaid, though—as long as Alex is one of the ushers. So when *are* you and Brian getting married? After his graduation or yours?"

Holly came slowly back to the present, smiling ruefully at her reflection in the mirror. Memories of the starry-eyed girl she'd been receded, leaving her looking at the thirty-four-year-old woman she'd become.

"Mom! Dinner!"

Holly snapped out of her reverie. "All right, Will! I'll be there in a minute!"

Her life had Will in it, and that was what mattered. There was no reason to fear a reminder of the past.

Still, seeing Alex again would be…strange.

She thought briefly about changing into something more—something less—something different. But—

"No," she said out loud. She wouldn't go to any trouble for a man who, as a boy, had never made a secret of despising her. Especially since the feeling had been mutual. With a resolute nod at her reflection, Holly left the bedroom and went downstairs.

Dinner with Will was fun, as meals in their house usually were, whether it included a group of friends or just the two of them. Under the influence of gooey cheese and laughing conversation, Holly felt herself relaxing.

This was nothing. A quick hello to someone she hadn't seen in years and would, hopefully, never see again. Thirty seconds and it would all be over.

This was nothing.

Right, Alex said to himself. Nothing. That's why he'd been standing outside the damn door for five minutes like some kind of idiot.

He turned away for a moment, resting his elbows on the porch railing and looking out at the front yard, where shadows chased moonlight through the trees.

Why was he making such a big deal out of this? He and Holly had never been friends. If anything, they'd been enemies. She was everything he'd hated in high school: uptight, conventional, all about rules and fitting in. The few times he'd tried to tell her there was more to life than playing it safe, she'd looked at him as if he was crazy.

Not to mention the fact that she'd dated his moron of a stepbrother all through school. That alone would have been enough to earn his dislike.

Fifteen years had gone by since then. And now, by some ridiculous twist of fate, he was standing outside Holly's front door, waiting to pick up her son. Brian's son.

Alex revised that in his head. Will wasn't just Holly's son or Brian's son; he was his own person, too. A terrific kid. A rare kid. The kind of kid a coach or teacher would always be grateful for and always remember.

His face softened as he thought about boys he'd worked with in the past, the boys he was working with now. They were all great kids in their own way. He had faith in all of them, even the ones no one else believed in.

He'd been a kid like that once.

Alex shook his head sharply. Enough with the trip

down memory lane. Tomorrow night was the first game of the season and Will Stanton was his backup quarterback, not to mention next year's starter if he fulfilled even a fraction of his promise. And Holly Stanton was just another parent.

He set his jaw, strode up to the door, and rang the bell.

"Coach is here," Will said, pushing back his chair.

All of Holly's calm evaporated. She had intended to go to the door with Will, where she would greet Alex with polite indifference. Instead she slipped into the dark living room, her heart beating ridiculously fast, so she could see the front hallway without being seen.

Before she could get a grip on her poise, Will was opening the door, and in the next second Alex McKenna stepped over the threshold.

Holly's breath caught in her throat. Just like in the old days, Alex seemed larger than life—and not just because of his size. His presence had always made everything else around him a little dimmer, a little duller, and fifteen years hadn't changed that.

On the surface, though, a lot of things had changed.

His hair was no longer bleached and spiked, for one thing. It was light brown, and cut fairly short. There was no safety pin in his left ear, no metal studs anywhere at all, and no black clothing. He wore a pair of khaki pants and a forest green button-down shirt.

The haircut and clothes together would normally come attached to a good boy. The kind you could safely bring home to Mother.

But the harsh planes of his jaw and cheekbones, the piercing blue eyes, the scar slicing through his left eyebrow—all these still screamed bad boy.

And all the conservative shirts in the world couldn't conceal those broad, muscular shoulders and rock-hard chest.

Sex, sin and danger. Yep, Alex McKenna was still open for business.

Alex grinned at Will and tried not to be too obvious about looking around for his mother.

The Stanton home, at least what he could see of it, was neat as a pin and furnished with quiet good taste. Big surprise there. Holly had probably been born with the Ralph Lauren logo tattooed across her forehead. The room to the right was dark, but just down the hall he could see the brightly lit kitchen, with lemon-yellow tile countertops and a red geranium on the windowsill. Good smells, like Italian food and freshly baked bread, came wafting toward him, but there was no sign of Holly.

Alex bit back an irrational feeling of disappointment. "Ready to head out, Will? I'm assuming you cleared it with your mom."

"Yep. She's right—" Will turned his head, but no one was there. "Well, she *was* right behind me...."

And then a small, slender redhead in an elegantly cut brown wool pantsuit came out of the shadows to stand beside her son. She looked up at him for a long minute, her head tilted to one side.

"Hi, Alex," she said finally, in the low, husky voice he remembered.

She was even more gorgeous now than she'd been as a teenager—and as a teenager she'd had every guy who saw her dragging his tongue in the dust.

Her face was the same—the same smooth, creamy

skin, the same delicate features. The expression in her green eyes was different: a little tougher, a little warier.

Her hair was exactly the same. Coppery red mingled with brown and gold, like fall leaves. She still wore it pulled back, although the style was a little more sophisticated now.

He could tell her lips were still full and soft, although right now they were pressed together, adding to the sense of caution reflected in her eyes.

And then there was her body. Hidden, naturally, behind a severely tailored suit that was obviously intended to play down her curves. Begging the question of why in God's name anyone would want to hide something so delectable….

Alex gave a mental shrug. Hell, he knew why she hid. She was still the same, play-it-safe Holly Stanton: afraid to put so much as a perfectly manicured toe on the wild side.

"Hello, Holly," he said. "Long time no see."

She was looking him up and down now, one eyebrow lifted. "You've certainly changed since I saw you last," she said, her voice amused.

Just like old times. In less than a minute, she'd managed to piss him off.

"The Gap just isn't a look I ever expected to see on you," she added.

The kicker was, he'd put on these damn clothes with her in mind. Thinking that maybe she'd see a different side of him. His jaw tightened. So much for a fresh start. Like the seventeen-year-old kid he'd once been, he wanted nothing more than to wipe that superior look off her face.

He leaned back casually against the door frame,

folding his arms across his chest. "Most of us change after high school, Holly. Except you, of course. *You* haven't changed a bit. Every hair in place…just like the old days." He grinned suddenly. "Of course, I did get to see another side of you once. The day I caught you dancing around that empty classroom, singing to Bruce Springsteen at the top of your lungs."

That got under her skin a little—he watched the heat come up into her face, the way it had when they were teenagers and he tossed a barb her way. Her eyes narrowed and she opened her mouth to say something, but a glance at Will made her hold it back. Alex wondered what she'd been about to call him.

"Wow, Mom," Will said, looking surprised. "I don't think I've ever seen you dance."

"That's because I don't," she said crisply. She looked from her son to Alex. "Not that this hasn't been fun, but don't you boys have plans to talk about that inflated rubber ball you're so obsessed with? Oh, and the pummeling," she added, the superior expression back. "Let's not forget the intellectual stimulation of the pummeling."

Will said goodbye to his mom and followed Alex out the door. "She's not exactly a football fan," he told his coach.

"Yeah, I picked up on that," Alex answered as he led the way to his car.

They were gone.

Holly closed her eyes and leaned back against the front door. "That went well," she said to the empty house.

Why had she let Alex get to her, as if they were still teenagers? Heck, she was the *mother* of a teenager, and a successful businesswoman to boot.

He said she hadn't changed a bit. She knew what that meant. Boring old Holly was still…boring.

Holly was suddenly filled with a desire to show Alex McKenna that she *wasn't* boring. That she could be sexy and wild and…dangerous.

She sighed. Who was she kidding? If she'd been uptight as a teenager—with one notable lapse—then how much more uptight was she now? Now that she was thirty-four, with a house and a son and a career to think about?

It was a little late in the day to start playing bad girl.

Not that she wanted to, Holly told herself as she went into the kitchen to clean up after dinner. She had a great life. A wonderful son, a beautiful home, and work as a financial planner she was good at and enjoyed.

Holly turned on the CD player she kept on the kitchen counter, and Bruce Springsteen's bedroom voice filled the air.

She had to laugh. Trust Alex to remind her of one of her more embarrassing teenage memories—getting caught pretending she was a rock star.

She remembered how much she'd hated it that Alex had been the one to see her looking so foolish. Alex never looked foolish. He was always cocky and self-assured, with a knowing expression that made her feel exposed. Like he could see right through her.

Everyone else accepted her at face value. She was Holly Stanton, honor student—a good girl who never gave her parents or teachers a moment of trouble. To Brian, she was the perfect girlfriend. Their marriage, which would take place after Brian finished law school and established his career, would be just like her parents' marriage: secure, successful and safe.

There was nothing safe about Alex. Their senior year he rebuilt an old Vincent motorcycle, all leather and chrome and sleek, powerful lines. Every so often he invited her to go riding with him. She could still remember his blue eyes daring her to do it even as his mocking smile told her she never would.

And she never did, of course. But a tiny part of her had always wondered what it would be like to get on that bike behind him, her legs pressed against his, her arms wrapped around his waist.

Holly came back to the present to find the sink almost overflowing with hot, soapy water. She turned off the tap quickly.

She hadn't been on a date in way too long—maybe that's why she was so susceptible to these memories. Why Alex had been able to get under her skin today. Yes, the man was annoying, but he was also gorgeous.

Sex on wheels.

She shook her head sharply and started washing dishes with vigor. No dates lately—that was her problem. She just needed to get out there again.

Holly bore down with her scrub brush to get the baked cheese off the lasagna pan. Maybe it would turn out to be a good thing she'd seen Alex again. Maybe it was just the push she needed to get out of her rut.

No, not a rut. She wasn't in a rut. She just needed to get out a little more, that's all. Everyone was always telling her that, even her own son. Maybe it was time she stopped laughing them off.

Holly rinsed off the now sparkling pan and set it in the dish drain. If she was going to embark on a quest to revive her love life, she might want to think about updating her wardrobe. At the moment, she had clothes to meet clients in and clothes to clean the house in. Nothing at all to drive men wild in.

On the other hand, that might be a little ambitious. Maybe she could start with clothes to make men realize she was female. Then she could sort of work up to driving them wild. She was a little out of practice, after all.

Come to think of it, maybe it would be better to forget the whole thing.

Alex felt good. He'd had a great skull session with his young quarterbacks, productive and upbeat. The entire team was raring to go for their opening game. The forecast for tomorrow was sunny and high sixties, perfect football weather, and Alex was starting to feel that rush he always experienced at the start of the season.

Alex glanced up at the Stanton house as he turned off the engine. He wouldn't go to the door this time. He had no desire to see Holly again, absolutely none.

"Nice job tonight, Will. Get a good night's rest and I'll see you tomorrow."

"Sure thing, Coach," Will said cheerfully as he slammed the passenger door shut behind him.

Time to go now, Alex thought as he slouched back in the driver's seat and looked at the Stanton home through his windshield. Will wasn't the only one who needed a good night's—

He froze.

The lights were on in a bedroom upstairs, and he could see Holly as clearly as if she were on stage. Her hands were in her hair, taking out whatever pins or clips held it in place. The next second it came tumbling down around her shoulders in a silky red mass.

She was wearing an old wool cardigan over the pants and blouse she'd had on earlier. She shrugged out of the cardigan, laying it on the bed behind her. Then she undid the top button of her blouse. And the next one.

He had about five seconds to make a decision.

Every cell in his body was screaming at him to stay. He might be honorable on the football field, but here? Hell, he was a man, not a saint.

Any other woman would let him into her house, into her bed, where he could see her up close and personal. Only Holly would never let him see her like this, and now he had an opportunity to catch a stolen glimpse. He'd be crazy to pass it up.

With a curse Alex turned the key in the ignition and pulled out of the driveway, his tires spitting gravel as he went.

When it came to Holly Stanton, crazy didn't begin to cover it.

Chapter Two

Why, Alex wondered as he drove home. Why couldn't he do what any sensible, red-blooded American male would have done?

It was just…she'd hate it so much if she ever knew he'd invaded her privacy like that. Not that she'd hate *him* any more—Alex doubted that was possible—but she was such a private person. Being watched like that, spied on, would really hit her where she lived.

He sighed as he let himself into his house. What was it about Holly? He'd dated all kinds of women—sexy, exciting women—and this one diminutive redhead could still tie him up in knots, make him feel like an adolescent hormone bomb.

He'd been a junior in high school when his family moved to Weston, a small town in Ohio northeast of Cincinnati. His stepbrother was a senior and, true to form, fit in at their new school right away. Equally true to form, Alex made it clear he had no intention of ever fitting in. He and Brian had always been at odds with each other. The only thing they'd ever come close to agreeing on was Holly Stanton.

Alex had met her first, since they were in the same grade. He could still remember walking into algebra that first day and seeing her at the chalkboard, writing out an equation, her teeth sunk in her lower lip as she concentrated.

It was as if all the air went out of the room.

A few weeks later he was coming out of detention (he'd earned seven in his first month, some kind of school record) when he heard music coming from an empty classroom. He opened the door and saw a boom box on one of the desks, and Holly Stanton dancing and singing with complete abandon.

He'd been struck dumb. She had a really good singing voice, sweet and smoky at the same time, and the bright copper waves of her hair bounced around her as she danced.

She caught him watching and stopped dead. He'd never seen anyone blush so deep or look so mortified.

"Don't be embarrassed, you have a great voice," he told her. Inspiration struck. "I'm starting a band with some kids at school. Do you want to be our lead singer? We practice every Friday. You could come this week if you want." In the world of a sixteen-year-old boy, there was no greater gift he could have offered.

Instead of being flattered, she looked hurt. "You're making fun of me," she said, turning away from him and shutting off the music. "And, anyway, I have plans on Friday. I'm going out with your brother."

"Stepbrother," Alex said through a spasm of jealousy that clenched his hands into fists. He had no idea she'd even met Brian. "You shouldn't go out with that jerk," he went on. "You deserve someone better than him."

She'd stared at him as if he was crazy. "Better than Brian? I don't think so."

During the next few weeks, Alex told himself it was only a matter of time before Holly saw through his stepbrother. She'd realize that Brian didn't care about her—that he'd never care about anyone but himself. She was smart. She'd figure it out.

But she didn't. And in school and at home he had to watch the two of them together, watch Brian swell with pride at having such a beautiful girl on his arm, the perfect accessory for his perfect life. And he had to watch Holly look to Brian for her cues, so anxious to be the perfect girlfriend that she could never relax, never be herself.

Was he the only one who really *saw* Holly? Not just that day he'd caught her singing, but in class, too, when her enthusiasm overcame her shyness and she talked about a book she loved or a topic she cared about. No one else seemed to pay attention to what she said—people were more interested in her looks, or in the fact that she was Brian's girlfriend. Was he the only one who really listened when she spoke up in class? The only one who noticed how funny and smart and passionate she could be?

The longer she was with Brian the more rare those flashes of enthusiasm became. She got quieter in general and especially around her boyfriend, letting him do all the talking. Letting him be the smart one.

Brian didn't want a girlfriend who was funny or

smart or passionate, who might take the spotlight off of him or challenge his complacence. What he wanted was a mirror, someone to reflect back his success, someone to cheer at his speeches and basketball games and awards ceremonies, someone to make him shine even brighter. And Holly seemed perfectly willing to play that role for him.

Watching her with Brian was like watching her disappear.

And there wasn't a thing he could do about it. What could he do, when she wouldn't listen to him? He tried a few times, in the beginning, but she shut him down fast. He might see behind her facade, but she didn't bother to look behind his. Holly had taken one look at him and decided he was a burnout, a troublemaker, and obviously not worth talking to.

He tried to hate her. He told himself he did hate her. But he'd never been able to ignore her. He fell into a pattern of baiting her, instead—needling her whenever he got the chance. And Holly had treated him like something on the bottom of her shoe.

Alex came back to the present, shaking his head. His feelings had been intense back then—he'd been a teenager, after all—but that was in the past. He wasn't that kid anymore, hadn't been for a long time. He was surprised his memories were still so vivid.

A lot of water had gone under the bridge since high school. Brian had moved out to California and was the rich, successful lawyer he'd always wanted to be. Holly was a single mom with a career of her own, and he was a high school football coach.

They were adults now. You'd think he and Holly would be able to start fresh after fifteen years. But after their brief meeting tonight, Alex doubted they'd ever be able to get along. They rubbed each other the wrong way and probably always would.

So why was he still thinking about her?

It didn't help that she was still so damn gorgeous—or that his body responded to her as if he were still sixteen.

He needed to get out more, that was his problem. Since moving back to Weston he'd been busy every weekend, either down at the school or fixing up the house. He needed to go out some Saturday night with a woman who found him charming and funny and incredibly sexy.

He wouldn't mind the company, either, he thought as he walked upstairs. His place was too big for one person. He didn't know what had possessed him to buy this old farmhouse, except that it had a great yard out back and he liked houses with character and history and projects to keep him busy in the off-season.

But a little company wouldn't hurt. Sexy, willing, female company. And soon.

It was Friday, the day of Will's season opener. Holly meant to go home after work and change for the game, but she got caught in a meeting at the end of the day and barely made it to the stadium in time for the opening kickoff. She felt distinctly overdressed in her peach silk pantsuit as she made her way through the crowd to the spot in the bleachers Angela and David Washington had saved for her.

The Washingtons were old hands at this, since their son, Tom, had been a star running back in his freshman year and this was his second season as a starter. Angela did her best to explain the game to her, but Holly could never figure out who had the ball, and she couldn't tell the players apart in their helmets and bulky uniforms. Still, she cheered when Angela and David did, which was often, and found enjoyment in the happy crowd, the kids' excitement and the beautiful September evening.

She'd spotted Alex right away, down by the players' bench. She noted objectively—at least she told herself it was objective—that he was looking very, very good in a pair of worn blue jeans and a Wildcats sweatshirt, his brown hair ruffled by the wind. She tried to focus on the game, but since she didn't really understand it and Will wasn't playing, it was hard to stay interested. She found her eyes straying to Alex instead.

He looked at home down there on the sidelines, talking animatedly to his assistant coaches, slapping his players on the back as he sent them into the game and giving them high fives when they returned, pacing back and forth as he watched the action on the field, arguing fiercely with an official over a disputed call.

The Wildcats must have been doing something right, because the score was thirty-one to seven near the end of the fourth quarter, when Alex sent Will into the game.

Holly's heart was in her throat as Will trotted onto the field to join the team huddle. Her hands gripped the cold metal seat when the players lined up, and when Will cocked his arm back to throw the ball. Then she gave the loudest cheer of her life when the pass was caught and the receiver crossed the goal line for a touchdown.

The game ended soon after that and Holly found herself swept onto the field with the hometown fans, family and friends swarming around the players in happy confusion. Holly took a few steps back as she searched for Will in the crowd.

When she felt a hand on her shoulder she turned, and when she saw Alex standing there, a bolt of electricity shot through her. She jerked away before she could stop herself.

"Nice game, Coach," she said lightly, trying to recover her poise.

"Thanks," he said, tilting his head to the side as he looked at her. "You know, I don't see a lot of silk suits and high heels at football games. Do you even *own* a pair of jeans?"

Holly flushed. "I came straight from work," she snapped. The two of them apparently couldn't talk without irritating each other, so why even pretend to be civil?

He was wearing that knowing smile of his, the one that said he knew he'd gotten under her skin. She was about to say a cold goodbye when Will came running up to them.

"Coach, we're taking you out to celebrate," he said jubilantly. "We're going to the Texas Grill, and you're the guest of honor." He turned to Holly. "A bunch of parents are going along, too. Won't you come, Mom? Please?"

Holly sighed inwardly. She'd never seen her son so excited—she had to celebrate with him. There'd be a lot of people there and it shouldn't be hard to stay away from Alex.

"Of course," she said, sounding as enthusiastic as she could. Will looked happy as he went back to his friends, but from the look Alex gave her before she turned away, she guessed she hadn't fooled him one bit.

Not that she ever had.

An hour later, having watched Will consume an enormous pile of barbecued spareribs and having eaten a few herself, Holly was watching Alex play pool. She had plenty of company—half the population of Weston seemed to be there, all of them wanting to congratulate the new coach. For tonight, at least, he was the most popular guy in town.

That sure was a change from high school. Back then, Alex had gone out of his way to alienate people. Now he was at the center of a warm circle of parents and kids, laughing and talking with everybody. He made a particularly spectacular shot, and one parent—a single mom like her, but looking ten years younger in a short denim skirt and shimmery top—took friendliness a step further by throwing her arms around Alex's neck and kissing him loudly on the cheek.

Okay, so some things hadn't changed.

Alex had always been a flirt. He never bragged about his conquests the way some guys did, but his relationships had always been…casual. Casual and numerous.

He was running the table now, amidst loud cheers. The single mom was cheering the loudest, and Holly felt a sudden wave of depression. She felt out of place in her work clothes, out of place in the midst of this boisterous, celebratory group.

She was just tired, that was all. It had been a long work week and she hadn't planned on going out tonight.

She found her son playing video games with his friends. "I'm feeling a little beat, honey. Do you mind if I head out now? I asked the Washingtons to drive you home so you don't have to leave the party early."

"No problem, Mom," Will said, giving her a quick grin before turning back to his game.

A few minutes later Holly was standing in the brightly lit parking lot, looking ruefully at her left rear tire. It was flat as a pancake. She remembered the broken glass in the stadium parking lot, which she'd thought she'd avoided.

Apparently not.

She thought briefly about going back inside for Will, but she knew he was still having fun. And, anyway, she was perfectly capable of changing a flat tire by herself. She'd been doing it for fifteen years.

She opened her trunk to get the spare.

Alex sat out the next pool game, but there was still a crowd around him—fans of the Weston Wildcats and parents bubbling over with enthusiasm for their sons' new football coach.

He was familiar with this kind of instant popularity. If they lost their game next week, it would just as instantly evaporate. But victory celebrations were always fun and he was enjoying himself, listening respectfully to one father's analysis of the game, when he caught sight of a familiar redhead walking away from the crowd.

"Absolutely," he said. "That's a good point about our pass defense. Now if you'll excuse me, there's another parent I need to say hello to."

He was determined to talk to Holly again tonight. On the drive over from the stadium, he'd decided to try one more time to have a normal conversation with her. The past shouldn't define the present. The relaxed atmosphere of the Texas Grill was the perfect setting—he could buy her a drink or challenge her to a game of pool. He refused to believe that two rational adults couldn't get past whatever friction still lingered from their high school days.

He saw her exchange a few words with Will, but before he could catch up to her she disappeared out the back door.

He paused, frowning. He thought about asking Will

completely as she moved the jack underneath the car and began to crank it up.

But when she was struggling to position the heavy spare over the wheel studs, he decided enough was enough.

"Okay, you've made your point. Now let me hold that up for you while you get it aligned."

She set the spare down for a moment and wiped her forehead with the back of her hand—her first sign of weakness. But when he moved to pick it up she slapped his hand away.

"No," she said. "I'm not a damsel in distress."

"I'm not trying to rescue you," he said in exasperation. "Just let me hold the tire while you fit it over the studs. Teamwork."

"I can do it myself."

"Come on, Holly. You're just being stubborn."

"I'd rather be…stubborn than…*helpless,*" she panted as she finally managed to get the wheel in position. It only took her a few more minutes to tighten the lugs and lower the jack.

"There," she said in satisfaction, tossing her tools in the trunk and using an old rag to wipe off her greasy hands. "That wasn't so hard."

"Right," Alex said, shaking his head. "Of course, you'd be halfway home by now if you'd just let me—"

"I can take care of myself, Alex. I don't need anybody's help."

Something else about her that hadn't changed.

The summer after their graduation, he'd heard that Holly was pregnant. He figured she and Brian would just step up their plans to get married and have the perfect yuppie life together. But when he found out how wrong he was, that Brian was turning his back on her, something inside him had snapped.

He'd broken Brian's jaw first. Then he'd gone over to her house and asked Holly to marry him.

It was crazy, of course. A white knight impulse that had hit him out of the blue. There'd been no reason in the world to think she'd say yes, and considering their history of mutual dislike, every reason to think she'd say no.

Still, her scornful refusal had stung.

Just like it did tonight. The stakes had been higher then, but the feeling was the same.

"I know you don't need my help, Holly. You've made that pretty clear. But that doesn't mean you can't accept it. What's so terrible about being rescued once in a while? Why are you so damn stubborn?"

She glared at him. "You're calling *me* stubborn? I told you I didn't need any help, but you insisted on staying out here, anyway. Why are *you* so damn stubborn?"

"Uh…guys?" It was Will, standing a few feet away.

How long had he been there? Alex glanced at Holly, who was looking as uncomfortable as he felt, and then back at Will, who was obviously confused by the tense conversation between his mom and his coach.

"So," Will said after a moment of awkward silence. "I guess you guys weren't best friends back in the day, huh?"

Holly took a deep breath and let it out again. "Not exactly," she admitted. "But that was a long time ago, and I'm sure we can keep from arguing every time we see each other now. Can't we, Alex?" she asked pointedly.

Not in this lifetime.

"Sure we can," he said out loud.

He glanced back at the restaurant and saw parents and their kids beginning to come out. "Is the party over already?"

"Well, yeah. You guys were out here a long time."

"It wouldn't have been so long if—no, I won't start." He shook his head. "Good night, Holly. Take it easy driving on that spare, okay? And, Will, I'll see you in practice next week."

Lying awake, staring up at the ceiling, Holly kept replaying Alex's words in her mind. What would it be like, she wondered. To let someone help her. To be rescued.

She hated herself for even asking the question. She'd been strong and independent for so long. The moment she let herself think about some man sweeping in and taking care of her, it would be over. She'd be lost. She'd be giving in to weakness, and it would destroy her.

She knew that. She knew it. And in case she was in any danger of doubting it, all she had to do was remember the day she'd gone to Brian with the news that she was pregnant.

Yes, it was unexpected. Yes, it was years sooner than they'd planned. But Holly had never doubted that Brian would support her, marry her now instead of after law school like they'd talked about. She'd gone to him trustingly, sure he'd take care of her and their unborn child.

It had been a long time since she'd thought about that day but the memory still hurt. The way he shouted at her that she was trying to ruin his life—his career.

He wouldn't have to quit school, she said. She could work part-time, and his parents might be willing to help. Her own parents hadn't taken the news well when she first told them, but they'd come around. And her grandmother would help as much as she could.

All she really wanted was to hear him say he loved her. That everything would be all right. That they'd figure things out together.

"If you go through with this, Holly, you're on your own. I won't have anything to do with you or the baby."

Holly could still remember the pain of that rejection. It had felt like the end of the world.

But it would never happen again. Because that was the last time she'd rely on someone else for any part of her happiness or welfare.

She hadn't spoken to Brian for four years after that. They seldom spoke now, although he saw Will once in a while. And she rarely spoke to her parents, who ended up kicking her out of the house after she refused to "take care" of the situation. They'd relented a few years later, asking to know their grandson, but Holly herself wasn't close with them anymore.

After Will was born, her friends had told her she should get a lawyer and sue Brian for child support. But she had refused. She had learned the one lesson that would become the cornerstone of her life: the only person you can trust is yourself. She wouldn't ask Brian for a damn thing.

Somehow she'd survived, even though she hadn't let anyone help her that first year or two—not her friends, not even her grandmother. Once she'd proven to herself she could stand on her own feet, she was able to accept her grandmother's love again, and be grateful for the way she doted on Will. And by that time Gran was nearly eighty and needed her almost as much as Will did, so Holly didn't feel as if she was in any danger of losing her hard-won self-reliance.

Except for Will, there was nothing more important to Holly than the independence she'd worked so hard to achieve. That's why she could never let herself fantasize about some man rescuing her…including Alex McKenna.

Especially Alex McKenna. He was already too dangerous to her sense of stability.

As maddening as he was, he was also one of the few people who could get past her defenses. He caught her off guard. Made her feel things. Her heart rate picked up whenever he was around.

Holly rolled her shoulders and tried to let go of some of the tension keeping her awake. So what if Alex had come back into her life? So what if he hadn't lost his uncanny ability to get under her skin, to make her question herself? She'd been doing just fine before he came back to town, and she'd continue to do fine, thank you very much.

She'd avoid him from now on, that was all. She'd go to Will's games but she'd stay away from Alex, and with any luck, he'd stay away from her, too.

She remembered how hard it had been to change that tire with him standing behind her, his presence making her hands tremble as she struggled to loosen the lugs. Knowing his eyes were on her had made the hairs stand up on the back of her neck.

She shivered now, thinking of those blue eyes. Then she thought of his chest, his shoulders, his smile, and her muscles turned to water. Damn her body, anyway. What kind of primitive programming made her stomach tie itself in knots whenever she saw him?

It didn't matter, she reminded herself firmly. Because from now on, she was going to stay away from Alex McKenna as if her life—or at least her sanity—depended on it.

Chapter Three

It would be a lot easier to forget about Alex if Will would stop talking about him day in, day out. How was she supposed to stop thinking about the man when he was her son's favorite topic of conversation?

The worst part was that the stories Will told made it harder to hate him. Will was a good judge of character, and he was crazy about Alex. Coach has such a great work ethic. Coach has so much integrity. Coach is so tough and smart and funny and—

It was Sunday afternoon, and Holly and Will were eating pizza in front of the TV and watching—big surprise—a football game. During the commercial breaks Will treated her to more rave reviews of Alex the Great.

"Mom, are you listening? Isn't that amazing? Don't you think Coach is—"

"Amazing?"

"Well, isn't he?"

Holly popped a mushroom into her mouth and licked tomato sauce off her fingers. "You bet. He's a paragon."

Will folded his arms and frowned at her. "Why do you always do that when I talk about Coach?"

"Do what?"

"The sarcasm. The eye rolling. Did you guys really hate each other that much when you were in high school?"

Holly sighed and leaned back against the sofa cushions. "Yes, we really did. Sorry. It's just hard for me to see Alex the way you do. When I remember the way he used to be."

Will looked interested. "So, what was he like back then? When you were teenagers."

Holly pulled the purple-and-yellow crocheted throw off the back of the couch and tucked it around her knees. Her grandmother had made it, and it always gave her a feeling of security.

"He was…irritating. So are you going to watch this game or what? 'Cause if not, I'm going to put on the financial news."

"Geez, Mom. If you don't want to talk about Coach just say so. You don't have to threaten me with unholy torture."

That Friday night, Will got to play for most of the second half. He completed seven passes, and Holly was pretty sure she'd never seen him so happy in his entire life.

Of course she also saw Alex, but she was getting used to that. Seeing him down there on the sidelines, fired up and intense, was becoming part of her Friday night routine—just like avoiding him was. But it was worth it to see Will so happy, so confident.

She wasn't ready to admit it yet, but she was actually starting to enjoy going to the games. She understood them better, for one thing, thanks to constant tutoring from her son. Then there was the crisp autumn air, the excitement of the crowd…and the fact that the Weston Wildcats were kicking butt.

Of course there was still a little too much pummeling for her taste, especially when her only child was on the receiving end of it. But still, all in all, Holly was starting to enjoy Friday nights.

So when a friend started off a sentence one day with, "I know you hate football, but—" she was surprised to hear herself say, "Oh, football's not so bad."

Gina looked at her skeptically over her turkey club sandwich. "Since when is football not so bad?"

Holly shrugged as she poured vinaigrette over her salad. "My son's on his high school team and he's sort of getting me into it. What were you going to say?"

"Well." Gina's eyes sparkled as she leaned over the table. "You know my fiancé?"

Holly raised her eyebrows. "Pretty well, yes. Considering the fact that I've worked with Henry for six years and actually introduced the two of you."

Gina grinned. "Okay, you get all the credit for my future marital bliss. And now I'm going to return the favor."

Holly took a bite of salad. "Uh-huh. And you'll be doing this how?"

"By fixing you up with your future husband, of course."

Holly sighed. "Gina, I love you, but we've been through this before. Do you remember the last time you fixed me up with my future husband?"

Gina waved it away. "Mark looked good on paper,

didn't he? Nice guy, stable job, easy on the eyes. I thought he was perfect for you. And you liked him in the beginning."

"Sure I did. And he liked me, too—until I cancelled a date one night when Will was sick. That's when he told me that Will would always come first in my life and I'd probably never get married. He also mentioned something about dying alone."

"Okay, so he turned out to be a jerk. He couldn't handle the fact that you're a single mom. But there are plenty of guys out there who can, and Will's older now."

Holly shook her head. "He still comes first. Mark was right about that. The truth is, I'm not looking for anything serious. That doesn't seem to work out for me. I just want to have a little fun. I haven't been out with anyone since Mark, and that was three years ago."

Gina looked surprised. "You want to have fun? I don't think I've heard you use that word before."

Holly wadded up her napkin and threw it at her. "If you think I'm so boring, why are you friends with me?"

Gina grinned. "Because you do my taxes for free every year. Now let's get back to your love life. If you want fun, we can do fun. We'll still go with my plan, only you'll date Rich instead of marrying him. Can I at least do my sales pitch?"

There would be no peace until she did. "All right, go ahead."

"He's really cute. Kind of a receding hairline, and he could stand to work out a little more, but definitely kissable. I happened to meet him because Henry's been his financial adviser for years, and they've gotten to be friends. He's the Bengals' play-by-play announcer."

She actually knew who that was, which meant she

was spending way too much time watching football with Will. "Rich Brennan?"

Gina looked delighted. "See? You've even heard of him. This is a match made in heaven."

Holly pushed her empty salad bowl away and reached for the dessert menu. "I'm a thirty-four-year-old single mother. He's a sportscaster on TV. Why would he want to go out with me?"

Gina glared at her. "Maybe because you're wonderful? Not to mention gorgeous? Henry and I ran into Rich the other day, and when he heard we were engaged he started talking about wanting to settle down, how he's done with the bar scene and playing the field and all that, and how hard it is to meet a nice woman. I told him my best friend is a beautiful redhead and the nicest person I know, and he asked if he could meet you. So what do you say?"

Here was her chance to walk on the wild side—or at least to go out on a date. Hadn't she been wanting to get out of her rut? And maybe Rich Brennan would turn out to be someone she could think about at night, alone in her bed when the lights were out.

Someone who wasn't Alex.

"Okay, I'll do it."

Gina breathed a sigh of relief. "I'm really glad you said that, because I already set it up. The Bengals have a bye week and Rich is free this Saturday. Now we just have to figure out what you're going to wear, since your own wardrobe is obviously impossible."

"My wardrobe is not—"

"Yes, it is," Gina said firmly. "We'll go shopping after lunch."

Holly sighed. "Fine. Now, can we talk about something important? Do you want to split the cheesecake or the chocolate truffle thing?"

It was Saturday night, and Alex was having a good time. The bar was hopping, and with the bye week most of his former teammates were there. Some of the Bengals cheerleaders were there, too, and he did a healthy amount of flirting. It was great to be back in Cincinnati for a night, great to hang out with the guys.

He also enjoyed listening to the girls commenting on the other patrons of the bar, including a well-known sportscaster who'd just picked up a karaoke mike to sing "Climb Every Mountain" from *The Sound of Music.*

"And, omigod, check out his date! He sure rebounded from Cherry in a hurry. Why does Rich always go for redheads? And where did he find this one? She's really pretty."

Alex glanced over at the table they were pointing at and nearly fell off his chair.

It was Holly Stanton.

What was she doing, laughing and clapping as Rich Brennan belted out a Julie Andrews song with alcohol-induced abandon?

"There's someone over there I've got to say hello to," he told the girls.

Alex made his way through the crowd toward Holly's table. She was sitting with her back to him, giggling at Rich's performance on the karaoke stage, and Alex wondered how much she'd had to drink. He'd never heard Holly giggle before.

He tapped her on the shoulder and she twisted around to see who it was. Her hair was loose tonight and it hung down her back in a rippling waterfall, framing her face in coppery waves.

"Alex!" she cried, rising to her feet and throwing her arms around him as if he were a long lost friend. For a few dizzying seconds she stayed like that, her slender curves pressed against him and her perfume surrounding him—something delicate, like roses—before she took a step back, swaying slightly.

His heart was pounding from the unexpected contact.

"Alex, Alex, Alex." She looked up at him solemnly, her lips parted. "I was thinking about you before, but now I can't remember why."

A curvy brunette came from the direction of the restroom. "Holly, who is this gorgeous man?"

Holly gestured with a flourish. "Gina, this is Alex. Alex, this is Gina. Gina's getting married soon," she said as a dark-haired man at their table tugged Gina down onto his lap. Gina planted a kiss on his forehead.

"That's Gina's fiancé," Holly said helpfully. "His name is Henry."

"Nice to meet you, Gina and Henry," Alex said before turning back to Holly. "So, how much have you had to drink tonight?"

"Not nearly enough," a familiar voice announced, and there was Rich, a guy Alex had known casually for years and had always liked. He slung a heavy arm around Holly's slender shoulders, and Alex found himself liking him less. "I'll know she's had enough when she lets me undo this button, and maybe a couple more. It's been driving me crazy all night."

He fiddled with the button in question, and Alex's jaw tightened. Holly smacked his hand away but she didn't seem very serious about it.

"It's nice to see you again, Alex," Rich said, holding out a hand. His other arm was still around Holly's shoulders. "What have you been doing with yourself since you left the league?"

"Coaching," Alex said, taking his hand briefly.

"Join us for a drink?"

"Don't mind if I do," Alex answered, taking a chair next to Holly after she sat down.

"So," he asked casually. "Are you two...dating?"

Rich was taking a long swig of beer, and it was Holly who answered him. "We met for the first time tonight. Gina fixed us up," she added, which made him think less kindly of Gina.

"It's about time Holly went out on a date," Gina said. "She's been living like a nun."

"What's wrong with that?" Alex asked, glancing at the woman in question. "If Holly wants to live like a nun, you shouldn't try to talk her out of it. There's nothing wrong with celibacy."

She was wearing a pair of jeans that hugged her hips, and a black cashmere sweater that was, thankfully, buttoned up to her neck. The curve of her breasts beneath the soft material was incredibly enticing, and if she'd been any other woman he would have sympathized with Rich's urge to undo a few of those buttons. But this wasn't just any woman, it was Holly. And he'd rather see her in full-body armor than with Rich drooling all over her.

Rich laughed loudly. "I know you're not speaking from personal experience. You're a great guy, Alex, but you're not exactly a shining example of the celibate lifestyle. I bet if we survey the crowd here tonight, we'll find at least twenty women who've been through Alex

McKenna's revolving door." He rose clumsily to his feet. "Now if you folks will pardon me, I've got to visit the little boy's room."

It was hard to believe he'd ever liked Rich Brennan.

Holly had picked up an empty beer bottle and was fiddling with the label, peeling it away from the glass. "You were like that in high school, too," she said. "A different girl every week."

"Were you ever one of those girls?" Gina asked, leaning back against her fiancé.

Holly looked horrified, and Alex winced.

"Of course not," she said. "We don't even get along. It's his fault," she added. "He's very annoying."

"Hey!" Her comment stung more than it should, even though he knew she'd had a few drinks. "I'm sitting right here. And I'm not the annoying one."

"Yes, you are," she said, twisting the label around her fingers. "You said I should be a nun. *That's* annoying."

Gina was no longer paying attention to them, distracted by something Henry was whispering in her ear.

"Okay, I take it back," Alex said, moving his chair closer to hers. "I don't think you should be a nun. So…how's the date with Rich going?"

Holly was tearing the label into pieces now, working methodically, a little crease between her brows. "All right, I guess," she said.

"Just all right?"

She bit her lip. "I don't…feel the way I thought I'd feel. The way I want to feel."

His heart skipped a beat, which probably made him a very bad person. He shouldn't be happy that Holly's date was a dud. "How do you want to feel?"

The label was in tiny silver pieces on the table. Holly

propped her chin on her hand as she thought about the question. "I don't know. I guess I was hoping for… magic."

Magic, he thought, remembering how his body had reacted when Holly had hugged him. "What would that feel like?"

She glanced at him. "Why are we talking like this? Like we're friends or something? We don't even like each other."

"Alcohol," he explained. "It's the great equalizer."

She considered that. "I've had three shots of tequila and two beers. When I stand up, the room kind of swoops." She blinked. "You know, it's possible that I'm drunk."

He held back a smile. "So what would magic feel like?"

She looked down at the table. "Well…goose bumps. Shivers. Your heart beating faster, your knees feeling weak. But I think I'm expecting too much."

She looked so vulnerable as she said that, her expression a little embarrassed, her cheeks turning pink. He wanted to tilt her chin up so she was looking right at him, he wanted to lean in close and—

I could make your knees feel weak, he thought.

On the other hand, maybe not. Holly had never given the slightest indication that she reacted to him the way he did to her. Besides which, they bugged the hell out of each other, which would seem to indicate a certain level of incompatibility. And on top of that Holly was a forever kind of woman, while he was a few-months-at-most kind of guy—as Rich had so considerately pointed out.

Still—"You ought to hold out for magic," he said gruffly. "You deserve magic. There's someone out there who'll make you feel that way."

She kept her eyes down, arranging the torn pieces of

label in a neat pile with a fingertip. "I don't know about that. Maybe I shouldn't shoot for the moon. I have Will, and I have friends, and I've got a job I love. That's pretty good, right? Maybe I'm not meant to have more."

Something about that quiet statement stabbed him through the heart. He started to tell her how wrong she was, but then he noticed Rich come out of the bathroom and lurch erratically toward the bar.

"Let me take you home," he said instead. He glanced at Gina and her fiancé, who were engaged in a long, slow kiss. "Your friends seem occupied, and your date is on his way to being unconscious. None of you should be driving tonight."

"I was going to take a taxi."

"Let me drive you."

Holly shook her head. "I know I haven't felt any magic yet, but Rich is sort of cute…and nice…and he seems interested. Maybe if I let things go a little further I'll start to feel something."

The idea of things going "a little further" between Holly and Rich made his whole body tense up. Rich rejoined them at that moment, handing a fresh beer to Alex and leaning down to nuzzle the back of Holly's neck. Alex gripped the bottle so hard he was surprised the glass didn't break.

"Did I mention how good you look?" Rich asked, reaching over her shoulder for Holly's top button again. Holly smacked his hand away again, but with less force than last time.

This was none of his business. In all the time he'd known her Holly had never asked for his help, and had never accepted it when it was offered. She'd never done anything but push him away. But he couldn't just leave her here like this, too drunk to make good decisions, her friends too drunk to realize it, and Rich too drunk to keep his damn hands to himself.

"You need to stop doing that," he said to Rich.

Even through the haze of alcohol, Rich heard the steel in his voice. He stared at Alex. Then he looked at Holly. "What's the story here?" he asked.

She blinked at him. "Huh?"

"Does Alex have some kind of claim on you?"

"A claim? On me? Of course not."

Rich turned to look at him again, and his expression was belligerent. "Back off," he said.

Alex got to his feet. "I'm taking you home," he told Holly.

"*I'm* taking her home," Rich insisted, putting a proprietary hand on her arm.

"Not in a million years," Alex said. He put a hand on the other man's chest and gave a quick, hard push that sent him stumbling backward several feet.

"Hey!" Holly said, jumping up. "I can take care of myself. And you're not the boss of me, Alex McKenna."

"For tonight, I am."

He put his hands on her waist and lifted her, amazed at how light she was. Then he threw her over his shoulder and strode out of the bar, ignoring the startled protests from her friends, from Rich and from Holly herself.

She was pounding on his back with her fists, but that wasn't as distracting as having so much of her pressed up against him for the second time that night. It was a relief when he got the passenger door open and could deposit her in the front seat, snapping her safety belt into place.

He was betting her advanced state of intoxication

would prevent her from getting out of the car before he could get in, and he was right. She was still fumbling to undo the belt when he slid in behind the wheel and turned the key in the ignition.

After a couple of minutes, she gave up.

"I'm going to be really, really mad at you once I'm sober again."

"I know."

"I can't believe you actually did that. Just…tossed me over your shoulder." She waved a hand in the air to emphasize her point and accidentally smacked him on the side of the head. He winced.

"And all because I was trying to have fun for once in my life," she grumbled, folding her arms and slouching down in her seat. "I know you think I'm uptight. You should be glad to see me loosen up."

"I don't mind you loosening up. I just mind you letting some drunken idiot unbutton your sweater in public."

"He's not an idiot. And I can take my clothes off if I want to. It's a free country."

"Fine," he snapped as he pulled onto the highway. "The next time I see you three sheets to the wind in the middle of a sports bar, you're on your own. Take off anything you want."

"All right, I will," she said. And before Alex had time to stop her, she grasped the hem of her sweater and pulled it over her head.

It was sheer luck that kept him from smashing into the truck ahead of them. He had one glimpse of creamy skin and apricot lace before he wrenched his eyes forward and got control of the car.

"Put your sweater back on."

"No."

"Dammit, Holly—"

"No."

He took a deep breath and let it out again. "Please put your sweater back on," he said more quietly. "Please?"

There was a moment of silence, during which Alex exerted every bit of his willpower to keep his eyes on the road. He was intensely aware of the woman sitting beside him, her chest rising and falling with each breath, her soft, bare skin just inches away. She smelled like tequila and roses, a strangely erotic combination.

"Okay," she said finally, tugging the soft black sweater back over her head. Alex wasn't sure if his relief or his disappointment was more intense.

"Thank you," he said, and meant it.

"That's all right," Holly said, and her voice sounded so resigned that he glanced over at her in surprise.

"What's wrong?"

She shrugged. "Nothing, I guess. It's just…you flirt with every woman you see, but when I took off my top you wouldn't even look at me. Do you think I'm repulsive or something?"

He couldn't believe what he was hearing. "Are you crazy? I—" He stopped himself before he could go too far. "I mean, it's not like that with us. We don't like each other, remember? You only took off your sweater because you're drunk. I'd never take advantage of you like that."

He wasn't sure she'd even heard him.

"I've never been any good at flirting. Or dating, for that matter." She rolled down her window and put a hand out to catch the night air. "I haven't had sex in three years. Three *years,* Alex. I think I've forgotten how."

What was she doing to him? If she was going to talk about sex he was going to have a hell of a time showing the restraint he'd just talked about.

And once she woke up tomorrow morning and remembered this conversation, she'd never talk to him again. He knew Holly—she wouldn't forgive him for seeing her guard down like this.

"Can I ask you a question?"

"Sure," he said warily, wondering what was coming now.

"Why did you leave the NFL?"

He glanced at her in surprise, and saw her looking at him curiously. Well, at least they weren't talking about sex.

He turned his eyes back to the road and tried to adjust to the change in topic.

"Why did I leave the NFL," he muttered. He glanced at her again. "I don't usually talk about that, but if you're sure you want to know—"

"I'm sure."

"Okay, then." He hesitated, remembering that time in his life. "Back when I was a pro athlete I got involved in a mentoring program with teenagers. I was working with this one boy, a really nice kid named Charles. He was a good student and a great football player. I worked with him for two years, right up until he got accepted to Michigan State. The day after he got the letter, he took twenty of his mom's antidepressant pills with a bottle of vodka and killed himself."

Holly gasped. "Alex, how awful. But…what did that have to do with you leaving the NFL?"

"After Charles died, his parents and I found out that he'd been using steroids. I didn't have a clue. He never talked to me about it, never said a word. He must have thought I was too much of a straight arrow to ask about something like that. And he was right—I never got into that crap. One of the many reasons is that it can affect your emotional balance, make you suicidal…especially if you're a teenager."

He took a breath. "I kicked myself for not seeing the signs. The acne, the mood swings, the way he bulked up so fast. But the fact is, I'd gotten used to seeing the signs. They were around me every day in the locker room. And even though I never did it myself, I turned a blind eye to it. It was just so much a part of the culture…as bad as it sounds, I started to take it for granted. After Charles died, I decided I didn't want a job where I could take something like that for granted. I decided I wanted to work with kids instead."

He grinned suddenly. "Or maybe I was just tired of getting beaten into the ground every Sunday. Either way, it was time to leave and I left."

Holly was looking at him thoughtfully. "I'm glad you left the NFL," she said after a moment. "I'm glad you came back here to Weston. I'm glad you're Will's coach."

He raised an eyebrow. "Well…thanks, Holly."

"Can I ask you another question?"

"Sure."

"Why were you such a jerk in high school?"

Now he raised both eyebrows. "Hey, who said I was a jerk?" He waited a beat, then shook his head. "Okay, even I don't buy that one. Yeah, I was a jerk. Most teenage boys are, you know. I hope you don't think Will is typical."

"No, I know he's not typical. But you weren't, either. I mean…I suppose most teenage boys are obnoxious, but you were…"

"More obnoxious than most? Maybe I was. Well—I hated my family, for one thing. One of the original excuses for teenage rebellion."

"Why did you hate them?"

"I never knew my real father—he took off before I was born. My mom died when I was eight and that left me with my stepfather. He and Brian never had much use for me, and I had even less for them. I wasn't related to them by blood, and they're the kind of people that matters to. I left home as soon as I could."

"So…you didn't really have a family. After your mom died, anyway."

He shrugged. "You don't have to sound so sad about it. I got over it a long time ago. And I've worked with kids who've gone through a lot worse." He glanced at her. "You went through worse."

She looked at him in surprise. "How did I go through worse?"

"Well…you always thought you had your parents' love. Didn't you? And they turned you away when you needed them most."

Holly ducked her head, and he wondered if he'd ventured onto forbidden ground. She had the excuse of alcohol for asking personal questions, while he had no excuse at all.

"How hard was it?" he asked gently.

She looked up again. "How hard was what?"

"Being on your own. In the beginning, I mean."

"Hard," she said, leaning back against the headrest. "But I got to watch myself getting stronger. It felt good to stand on my own two feet, to take care of myself and Will without owing anything to anybody." She turned her head to look at him. "Does that make sense?"

"Yeah," he said. "That makes a lot of sense." He hesitated. "You know, Holly…I never told you this, but I've always admired you like hell for what you did. For making a life for yourself and Will like that, out of nothing."

She tilted her head to the side and started to smile. "Wait a second. Was that a compliment?"

"Don't let it go to your head. I still think you're too stubborn and that you make things hard for yourself when you don't have to. But I do admire you, even when you're frustrating my chivalrous instincts."

"The man calls *me* stubborn," she said as if to herself, shaking her head. But when Alex shot a glance at her, he saw that she was smiling.

She reached a hand out into the night wind again. "It's my turn to ask another question now."

"Fire away."

"Why did you carry me out of that bar?"

He made a left turn onto Holly's street. "I've known Rich a long time," he said after a moment. "He's an okay guy, but he's not right for you. I've seen him go through hundreds of women."

"Well, so do you," Holly pointed out. "Don't you?"

"Not *hundreds*," he said evasively. "And I don't go around breaking hearts. I'm always clear up front that I don't want to get serious."

"And that makes it okay?" She shook her head. "Admit it, you're just as bad as Rich. But I don't care if he plays the field. I don't want to pick out china patterns or anything—I just want to go on a date. I could use the practice."

"You can go on all the dates you want. Just not with Rich."

She folded her arms and lifted her chin in the air. "You can't tell me what to do."

"Maybe not," he conceded as he pulled into her driveway, "but I can call up my old pal and warn him that if he goes near you again I'll beat him to a pulp."

"Alex! You wouldn't do that."

"You bet I would. And I will, too." He turned off the ignition. "As adorable as you look with your nose stuck in the air like that, it's my duty to tell you that you are now home."

In the sudden dark and quiet, Holly turned to look at him. "You think I'm adorable?"

He looked back at her for a minute, and then got out of the car. If he stayed there one more second he wouldn't answer for the consequences.

"You said I was adorable," she reminded him when he opened her door.

"Like a golden retriever puppy," he said as he helped her out.

"Wait a minute. Now I'm a dog?"

"A really cute dog. Haven't you ever seen a golden retriever puppy?"

He walked her to her front door. "Good night, Holly," he said, but it felt like goodbye. He knew he wouldn't be this close to her again.

"Good night, Alex," she answered, but she stayed where she was.

Time to go, he reminded himself. Except he couldn't seem to move.

He reached out to tuck a stray curl behind her ear, and then did what he'd been wanting to all night. He ran his fingers slowly through the lustrous red silk of her hair.

As soon as he did, he wished he hadn't. Now he knew it was even softer than he'd imagined, and that was not going to help him sleep tonight.

"That felt nice," she said, sounding surprised. She rolled up her sleeve and showed him her arm. "Look! You gave me goose bumps."

Really time to go.

Only those big green eyes of hers were holding him there, and for once they weren't narrowed with suspicion or dislike. Her lips were parted slightly as she looked at him, and if she were any other woman, drunk or not, he would have kissed her.

When the moment stretched out a little too long and he felt himself leaning toward her, he reached past her instead and opened the door.

"You should go inside," he said. "Take some aspirin before you go to sleep."

"Aspirin? But I feel great!"

"Not tomorrow morning, you won't. That's when you're going to wake up sober and be really, really mad at me. Remember?"

"Right," she said, nodding. "Only, I can't remember now why I was so mad at you."

He smiled crookedly. "Don't worry—I'm pretty sure it'll come back to you."

Chapter Four

Somebody's head was hurting. Holly felt really bad for whoever it was, because the pain was a kind of throbbing, pounding—

"Mom! Aren't you awake *yet?*"

Holly winced. As she'd begun to suspect, the headache belonged to her. "Don't shout, Will."

"I'm not shouting. I think you have a hangover."

Holly groaned and rolled over in bed, keeping her eyes closed.

"You should worry about the example you're setting for your impressionable son."

"Have some pity, Will. Your voice is going right through my head. What's left of it, anyway."

"Okay, okay. I think you're supposed to take Vitamin B and drink lots of water. I'll make you some coffee, too. Wait right here."

What did he think she was going to do? Hop out of bed and skip down the stairs, whistling a jaunty tune?

She opened her eyes, staring up at the ceiling and praying for death. Instead she got Will, back way too soon, carrying not coffee but the cordless phone.

"It's Coach," he said, sounding surprised. "He says he wants to talk to you." He set the phone down on the bed next to her and went back downstairs.

Oh, God.

Memories of last night came flooding back, and she stared at the phone as if it was a snake about to bite her. The knowledge of who was on the other end made her feel ill.

Well, more ill.

She'd done a striptease in his car and he hadn't even looked at her.

When she thought about the sweater incident she felt hot all over, and not in a good way. When she thought about the conversation in the bar and then on the drive home, she felt worse. And when she thought about how close she'd come to kissing him on her front porch, she pulled the covers over her head and prayed that somehow, some way, she'd be beamed off the planet and onto the bridge of the Starship Enterprise.

The only thing that kept her from throwing the phone out the window was the knowledge that if she didn't answer it, Alex would know exactly why. He'd know she was too embarrassed to talk to him.

Holly threw off the covers, picked up the phone and hit the talk button.

"Why are you calling me at dawn?" she asked as crisply as she could.

She could hear him laughing softly over the phone line. "It's noon, Holly."

She glanced at the clock and saw he was right. She groaned, and heard him laugh again.

"Okay, then, why are you calling me at noon?"

"I wanted to see how you were feeling. And I wanted to see if you were still talking to me."

She hesitated. "I feel like crap. Thanks for asking."

"I'm sorry to hear it." A short pause. "And what about my second question? Are you still talking to me?"

She bit her lip. The simplest thing, she decided, would be to play dumb. If he had any decency at all, he'd go along with her.

"Why wouldn't I be?" she asked innocently. "Of course I'm still talking to you. I mean, as much as we ever talk to each other."

There was another pause. "So that's how you're going to play it," he said. "I should have known."

Her grip on the phone tightened. "What do you mean?"

"You know exactly what I mean. You're going to pretend none of it happened."

"Well, what's wrong with that? Why wouldn't I want to forget last night? I was drunk, Alex. If you were a gentleman, you'd forget about it, too."

"A gentleman? If I wasn't a gentleman, I—" He stopped abruptly.

"What?" she asked, daring him to finish the sentence.

"Let's just say you seemed—receptive."

"If I seemed receptive, it's because I was drunk," she said coldly. "Because I am *not* receptive. Not to you, anyway. And I never will be. You're pushy and arrogant and you throw women over your shoulder like some kind of Neanderthal. I could never be interested in someone like you."

"Right, of course. I obviously don't meet your high standards for men. Like Brian, the disappearing father. Or Rich, who would have slept with you for a couple of weeks and then dumped you."

A wave of anger made her sit straight up in bed. "How dare you judge me? I don't see you in any perfect relationship. In fact, I'll bet you've never been in a relationship."

"I've been in plenty of—"

"I'm not talking about sex. Tell the truth, Alex. Have you ever been with one woman for more than three months? Have you ever gotten to the stage where you left a toothbrush at her place?"

There was a pause. "Just because I haven't found the right woman yet doesn't mean I—"

"Oh, come on, Alex. You're in your thirties. You're never going to find the right woman. I bet you don't even want to. You're perfectly happy playing the field. And hey, it's a free country. I don't care what you do in your personal life. But you've got no right to judge me, and you had no right to carry me out of that bar last night. I'm a grown woman, and if I want to have some fun with a guy I just met that's my business. If I want to have a wild affair with him, that's my business, too."

There was a longer pause.

"Fine," Alex said coldly. "Forget I said anything. It's obviously impossible to do you a favor, so I won't. Good luck with the wild affair by the way. Of course after a three year sabbatical you might be a little rusty—"

"Okay, that's it. You know, Alex, in my alcohol-induced fog last night there were actually three or four minutes where I didn't feel like killing you. Those minutes are now officially over. Goodbye."

She hung up without waiting for a response and fumed. After a few minutes she threw off the covers and got out of bed so she could fume while pacing back and forth. Much more satisfying.

"Hey, you're up," Will said, coming into the room with a tray that held, thankfully, nothing but a glass of water, a mug of coffee, a vitamin pill and two aspirin.

"What did Coach want?" he asked as he set the tray down.

"Nothing," Holly said. She downed the vitamin and aspirin with big gulps of water. "Thanks for this, by the way. Did you have breakfast?"

"Sure, I had breakfast." He frowned suddenly. "That reminds me. When I was down in the kitchen there was this smell—like burning or melting or something. It was pretty faint and I couldn't tell where it came from. It might have been my cooking, but do you think we should have it checked out? In case it's something electrical."

Holly sipped her coffee. "It's probably the oven. I've been meaning to give it a good cleaning. I'll go down later to check."

"Okay. Is it all right if I go over to Tom's house today? We're working on that social studies project together."

"Of course. I'll enjoy a Sunday afternoon without football for once."

"I'll see you tonight, then, around nine o'clock. Tom's parents invited me to stay for dinner if that's okay."

"Sure thing. Have fun."

"I will, Mom. Don't forget to check out that smell in the kitchen."

"I won't."

But she did forget. She didn't go near the kitchen at all that day, not feeling hungry in the afternoon and developing a sudden craving for fast food at dinner time, which she decided to indulge. She went to bed early, even before Will got home.

He didn't stop by the kitchen, either. He'd eaten a huge dinner with Tom's family and had no appetite for his usual late-night snack. Like his mom he went to bed fairly early, around ten o'clock. So both of them were sound asleep when the fire came through the wall, tongues of flame licking their way into the house, feeding eagerly on the two-hundred-year old woodwork and antique furniture and growing from a whisper to a roar.

The smoke alarms went off, but Holly was sleeping so soundly she didn't wake up right away. There was so much smoke in her room already that she might easily have never woken up again.

When she did, gasping and then coughing, she realized in one horrified second what was happening.

Will, she thought frantically. She stumbled out of bed and ran into the hall, her eyes smarting and her lungs desperate for clean air. But over the banister she could see an orange glow, hear the fierce roar—and instinctively, she knew they only had seconds to get out.

She flew into Will's room and shook him roughly awake.

"What's going on?" he asked groggily, and then he gasped and coughed just like she had.

"Fire," she said sharply, going to his window and throwing up the sash and the screen and looking down at the ground below.

"Out," she ordered, turning to face him. He was standing up now, looking terribly young in his pajamas, but holding his jaw firm and trying to control his fear.

"You first, Mom. I can't just leave you here!"

"*Now*, Will. I mean it. I'll be right behind you. The ground slopes up on this side of the house so the drop won't be so bad, but try to land as softly as you can. When your feet hit the ground, let yourself collapse to absorb the shock."

Will nodded wordlessly. He went over to the window and sat down awkwardly on the sill, maneuvering his long legs through the opening so they dangled outside, his hands braced on either side of him. He hesitated a moment and then dropped. Holly heard him grunt as he landed.

Holly followed almost immediately. She angled herself to one side, not wanting to land right on top of her son, and crashed into a rosebush. She hardly felt the pain of the deep scratch to her forearm and the one across her face.

For a moment she lay still, fighting to get her breath back. Will had scrambled to his feet and stood looking at the house he had lived in most of his life. It was burning fast, going up like tinder, and the flames were everywhere now. Holly could feel the heat, and a sharp, acrid smell was in her nostrils.

"The fire department," Holly said. "We've got to call the fire department." Even as the words came out of her mouth they heard sirens in the distance, coming closer.

"I think someone already called them," Will said. He sounded dazed, and Holly struggled to her feet.

"I want you to go next door to Mrs. Hanneman's," she said. "I'll stay and meet the firemen. I want to make sure they know we both got out, so they don't send anyone in there."

"All right, Mom," Will said, sounding obedient, like a little boy, and Holly's heart beat painfully as she watched him walk across the lawn to the neighbor's house.

Mrs. Hanneman was already outside, standing on her porch in a long flannel nightgown, staring at the Stanton home in obvious horror. She went running down the steps when she saw Will coming toward her and threw her arms around him.

Holly walked slowly away from the burning house, toward the street, noticing when she got there that several of the neighbors were in their front yards or on their porches, watching the disaster unfold in their midst with their hands pressed to their mouths, frozen with shock.

The first fire truck came screaming to a stop in front of the house. Holly forced her legs to move faster, to meet the firemen who came pouring out onto the sidewalk. "There's no one inside," she shouted to the first one she came to.

He looked down at her. "Is it your house, ma'am?" he asked loudly, over the roar of the fire and the wailing of the sirens.

"Yes. It's just me and my son, and we both got out safely. We don't have any pets. Please don't send any of your men in there!"

The fireman nodded. "Make sure you stay clear, ma'am. When the paramedics come, you and your son should both be checked out, just in case."

"Okay," she said faintly, but the fireman, faceless in his uniform, was already gone, running to help with the heavy hose.

I should go check on Will, Holly thought, her mind working in slow motion and her body numb. She started to walk but she couldn't feel her legs. The horrible sounds all around her—the greedy flames, the screaming sirens, the shouts of the firemen— seemed to recede.

There had been beautiful glass in her grandmother's home. The stained glass above the front door, the chandelier in the dining room, the diamond-shaped panes in the bathroom windows upstairs. Holly walked past Mrs. Hanneman's without stopping, making a wide circuit around the neighbor's house until she reached the big backyard.

It was oddly private back there. No horrified neighbors, no firemen. Holly stood watching the blaze, blinking, and then suddenly her legs gave way and she was crouching on the ground, retching, her whole body racked with the force of her dry heaves.

Alex couldn't sleep. He'd called Rich to apologize about the night before, and to make his feelings known on the subject of his ever going out with Holly, but the sportscaster just laughed.

"Are you kidding? As soon as you tossed her over your shoulder I knew she was off the market. I bet you've never done anything like that in your life. You've got it bad, huh? I guess she's the reason you haven't been in Cincinnati much lately."

Alex frowned at the phone. "Holly and I are not a couple. I just don't want you going after her. She's not like the girls you usually pick up. She's…different."

"Sure she's different. Because you've got a thing for her."

"I don't have a thing for her."

"Uh-huh. Well, it was nice knowing you, buddy. Invite me to the wedding, okay? I always get lucky with bridesmaids."

A few hours later Alex lay in bed, restless and edgy, as far from sleep as he'd ever been in his life. Finally he gave up the fight and turned on his bedside lamp, reaching for his current issue of *Sports Illustrated*. He hadn't read more than a paragraph when the phone rang. He grabbed the receiver off the cradle.

"Yeah," he said.

"Coach! It's Tom Washington."

Alex glanced at the clock in surprise. "It's almost midnight, Tom. What's going on?"

"It's about Will," he said, and Alex tensed. "His house, actually. You know my dad's a fireman, right? He just got called out to a fire—at the Stantons. A bad one."

A chill ran through Alex's body. "Do you know if they're okay?"

"I don't know anything yet except that it's bad. Coach, can you pick me up and take me over there? My mom's working the night shift at the hospital and I—"

"I'll be there in five minutes. Wait for me out front."

Alex threw on some clothes and cursed viciously as he tried to tie his sneakers with shaking hands. He fought to stay calm as he drove to Tom's, knowing that it wouldn't help Holly any if he wrapped himself around a tree.

Tom was waiting at the curb, and he jumped into the car and slammed the door almost before it came to a stop. Alex saw he was holding a small transistor radio and figured it was tuned to the fire department's band.

"Any news?" he asked as he pulled away and headed for Holly's house.

Tom shook his head. "Just that one guy said it was the worst fire he'd seen in five years."

Alex felt cold. "Anything about the Stantons? If they got out safely?"

Tom shrugged helplessly. "I'm not sure. I can't always follow what they're saying. I *think* someone said there wasn't anyone inside the house…."

They turned down Maple Avenue, and both of them gasped. The rising flames, the smoke, the flashing lights and wailing sirens, the people—

There was an ambulance there, too. Alex parked across the street and he and Tom ran over to the paramedic leaning against his vehicle.

"Anyone hurt?" Alex demanded, his voice sharp with fear.

The paramedic shook his head. "They both got out. A mother and a son. No burns or serious injuries. I've already seen the boy and he's fine. I'm still waiting for the mother, just to check her over, and to make sure all the men are okay." He glanced at the raging inferno that had once been a home. "It's a bad one, all right. But no one was hurt."

Alex closed his eyes. "Thank God," he breathed. He opened his eyes. "Where are they?"

"The boy's over there," the paramedic said, pointing toward the house next door, where Tom and Alex could see Will on the front porch, leaning against the railing and watching the fire. An elderly woman stood next to him with her hand on his shoulder. Tom took off at a run while Alex turned back to the paramedic.

"And Holly? The boy's mother?"

"She's definitely okay—she talked to one of the firemen when they first got here. I'm not sure where she is now. Maybe with another one of the neighbors."

Alex scanned the street and didn't see her anywhere. He tried to think clearly. If she wasn't with Will, she wouldn't be with a neighbor. If she wasn't with Will it meant she didn't want to be with anybody. Where was she? Off by herself, watching her home go up in smoke? She was in shock, emotional if not physical. He had to find her.

On a hunch he headed for the backyard, passing close enough to the house that he could feel the heat from the crackling flames.

Alex quickened his pace. Thank God, there she was. She was wearing a long white nightgown and was down on her hands and knees, retching. In an instant Alex was at her side, holding back her hair, although she didn't seem to be throwing anything up. After a minute the terrible convulsions eased and Holly rocked back on her heels, shuddering. Alex knelt down beside her and checked for injuries.

"You're bleeding," he said, his voice shaking. He used his sleeve to wipe the blood from her face. "It's just a scratch," he said, weak with relief. "This one, too." He cradled her forearm as he gently cleaned away the blood. "We need to get some antiseptic on these," he said. Holly didn't respond, and Alex wasn't sure she'd heard him. He wasn't sure she knew he was there. Her eyes were wide and dark as she stared over his shoulder at her house, her face lit by the garish light of the flames.

"Holly," he said softly, trying to reach her. "Holly," he said again, cupping her face in his hands and moving so he was blocking her vision, blocking the sight of the fire. Her frozen stare finally wavered, but she still didn't see him.

"My fault," she said, so softly that Alex almost missed it.

"What do you mean?" he asked gently, stroking the hair away from her soot-streaked face.

"This is my fault. Will noticed something in the kitchen, a smell that worried him. I told him I would check it out. I didn't. I had a hangover, and I forgot. It must have been the wiring in the kitchen. I'm the mom, it's my job to—oh, God, I'm the mom—what a joke, what a damned joke—"

She started to shake, and Alex pulled her into a rough hug. "This is not your fault, Holly." Her face was buried against his shoulder, and for just a moment the tension holding her body rigid eased a little. But then she jerked upright, pushing him away from her.

"It *is* my fault," she said harshly. "I got drunk last night and I was hungover today and I didn't pay any attention to what Will was saying. He could have died in that fire because of me. Because I was careless and irresponsible. I don't get to make mistakes, Alex. I'm the only parent Will has. Of course it's my fault."

Alex gripped her shoulders. "Stop it, Holly. Stop blaming yourself."

"My mattress," she said, staring toward the house again. Alex glanced back over his shoulder and saw that the firemen had managed to contain the blaze. No sign of a mattress, though.

"What are you talking about, Holly?"

"It's brand-new. I just bought it. Oh, God, my mattress!" She struggled to her feet and watched the firemen douse the last of the flames, leaving a blackened, smoking ruin. "There's nothing left. It's all gone. Everything that belonged to my grandmother. All the beautiful things she made."

Her voice sounded numb, dazed, and Alex wanted so much to help her it was like an ache in his gut.

"Will's baby pictures. All our photo albums. All our—"

Alex listened helplessly as she recited the litany of loss in a dead voice. "I know it's terrible," he said, wincing at the inadequacy of his words. "But you and Will are safe, Holly. Try to focus on that. That's all that really matters."

Holly turned to look at him, and for the first time since he'd found her behind the house Alex felt like she was actually seeing him.

"Safe," she repeated. "Safe." She backed away a couple of steps and gave a bitter laugh. "Sure, right, we're safe." She stood still for a moment, her eyes on him with something unreadable in their depths. When she spoke again her voice was cold and remote. "You must really be enjoying this, Alex."

His head snapped back as if she'd punched him in the face.

"What?"

"You heard me. This must be your idea of heaven."

He stared at her. "How can you say that? How could you even think it? You think I enjoy seeing you—"

"Vulnerable? Yes, I do." A spark of anger flared up in her eyes, and Alex told himself that any emotion was better than the empty, terrible numbness he'd seen in her a moment ago.

"You always show up when life hits me in the face, don't you? It's your favorite sideshow. I'm stuck-up and condescending and holier-than-thou, right? Just ripe for a fall. And you love it when that happens, when I get knocked down. Or knocked up, as the case may be."

Alex looked at her warily. "Holly, you're not making sense right now. You're in shock. It's good to let out the pain you're feeling, but—"

"All through high school you wanted me to screw up, to make a mistake, to stop being 'Little Miss Perfect' or whatever else you called me. Not to mention you spent two years telling me what a jerk Brian was. You couldn't wait to say I told you so. And then you hit the jackpot. You found out I was pregnant and you came straight to my house to rub my face in it."

Alex's jaw tightened as he remembered that night. His stammered, eager proposal and her scornful rejection. "I asked you to marry me, Holly."

Holly laughed bitterly, turning her eyes away. "Right, of course. What better way to point out the fact that I was going to be an unwed mother?"

Alex strode forward and grabbed her roughly by the shoulders.

"Holly, I asked you to marry me because I wanted to take care of you and the baby you were going to have. I wanted to kill Brian for turning his back on you—and when I thought about how scared you must be—"

"You didn't want to miss it, right? You wanted a front row seat."

"Stop saying that! I wanted to help you. You didn't want my help. You're so damn stubborn, so determined to be independent at all costs, sitting up on that pedestal where you don't need anything from anyone—"

"And you'd like nothing better than to knock me off

that pedestal. Right?" She cocked her head to the side
and tilted her chin up, as if presenting an easy target.
"So take your best shot."

He stared at her. With her breath coming hard and
fast and her fists clenched at her sides, she definitely
looked like a woman on the edge. "Listen to me, Holly.
You're in shock right now with everything that happened tonight, and I know this isn't about me. But you
have to believe I can't stand seeing you in pain. You
want the truth? It's just about killing me. Even back in
high school I never wanted to hurt you. Not really."

"Is that right?" Holly said softly. Her face was in the
shadows, but by some trick of the light her eyes were
glittering like a cat's. "You never wanted to hurt me.
Well, that's interesting. Because you did." Her voice
was trembling and she took a breath. "You've always
hurt me, Alex. But now *I'm* going to hurt *you.*"

He saw the punch coming before she threw it. He
saw it coming, and he didn't even try to defend himself.

"Mmff," he said as she connected with his jaw.

His plan was just to absorb the punishment until
Holly had burned off whatever steam she needed to.
What the hell, he thought with grim humor, if this was
what she needed right now at least he could give it to
her. He'd never been able to give her anything else.

But after that one wild swing, Holly stared at him in
horror. Her hand went to her mouth. "Alex," she said,
her voice breaking. "Oh, God, Alex, I'm so sorry."

"It's okay, Holly," he said quickly.

"Alex, I—"

"Don't worry," he said, hoping she wouldn't feel
guilty about this on top of everything else. "You've had
a rough night and you were burning off some steam.

I've already forgotten all about it. Or at least I will when the feeling comes back to my face."

"No," Holly said with sudden determination. "You have to let me apologize. Not just for punching you, although that was bad, but for the things I said…the horrible things I said."

Tears welled up in her eyes and Alex couldn't stand it. He did what he'd been wanting to do since he'd first found her tonight. He gathered her into his arms, holding her tight, murmuring something wordless and soothing into her hair.

He was amazed at how perfectly they fit together. He found himself wishing he could protect her like this forever, shielding her from the world with his body, so that nothing would ever hurt her again.

And this time she relaxed into him.

"Why do we do it?" she was asking, her voice muffled against his chest but still audible. She pulled her head back slightly, enough so she could look up at him. Her face was streaked with dirt and blood and tears, and her hair smelled like smoke, and she was still the most beautiful woman he'd ever seen.

"Why are we so awful to each other? Because it's not just me, you know," she went on, with a little of her old spirit. "I mean, I definitely get the prize tonight, but you can usually hold your own. Why do we do it? Are we really so immature that we can't let go of feelings we had when we were teenagers?"

She started to brush away her tears with the back of her hand, but Alex stopped her. He used his sleeve instead, wiping her face gently, and when he was done Holly's arms tightened around him and she rested her cheek against his chest.

Alex was suddenly and uncomfortably aware that he wasn't just a human being offering comfort to someone in pain, but also a man holding a woman he was wildly attracted to. His heart was hammering, and it would have been so easy to let his comforting caresses become something more. To crush her mouth to his and kiss her until she couldn't think straight, until passion drowned out her pain, even if it was only for a moment.

Except that Holly didn't feel what he felt. And even if she did, he couldn't imagine a more inappropriate moment to give in to his attraction.

He pulled back from her a little under the guise of carrying on a conversation.

"I don't know why we do it," he said, tipping her chin up so he could look into her eyes. "But it doesn't matter. We can change all that starting now. We'd better, because you and Will are coming to my house tonight. And you'll be staying with me for as long as you need."

His vocal cords were obviously leading their own life, because his brain was shouting *noooooo* even as he made the offer.

Not because it would be any big inconvenience. Giving up his privacy would be a little tough, but he could handle it. And he really wouldn't mind having Will around. Hell, he'd enjoy it.

But invite Holly to live under the same roof with him? The woman who fired his blood and starred in his fantasies and who, right this moment, looked like an extra from a disaster movie and could still inspire lustful thoughts? Most importantly, the woman who wouldn't feel the same way about him if he was the last man on earth?

He had to be out of his mind.

* * *

He had to be out of his mind. Holly blinked up at him, wondering if he was serious. Maybe the easiest way to find out was to ask.

"Are you serious?"

She thought she saw him gulp. "Of course I'm serious," he said quickly. "Why wouldn't I be?"

"Well, for one thing, there's a really good chance that if we live under the same roof we'll end up killing each other."

Alex brushed that possibility aside. "Don't be silly. Didn't you notice the major breakthrough we just had? We got over the whole enemies thing. We're friends now."

"Friends?" she repeated thoughtfully, liking the sound of it. "I don't know, Alex. It seems like a pretty big leap to go from enemies to friends. You really think it's possible?"

"I think that in a world where a hundred-pound woman can throw a punch like Mike Tyson, anything is possible."

Holly took a deep breath. This was all so strange. Her home burning to ashes behind her, and Alex McKenna offering comfort. And the way they were talking to each other… It felt comfortable, like they'd known each other a long time. Which they had, of course. Just not as friends.

"I weigh a lot more than a hundred pounds."

He stepped back and made a show of appraising her body, and Holly felt a sudden shiver pass through her that had nothing to do with the cold. Maybe staying with him wasn't such a good—

"Okay, maybe a hundred and ten. Now, I think it's about time you and Will come home with me where there's a shower and a bed. What do you think?"

His blue eyes were asking her to accept his invitation, and against her better judgment, she nodded yes. He looked relieved, which probably meant he wasn't regretting the offer. Not yet, anyway. And Holly did like the idea of taking Will to the home of someone he liked and trusted.

Liked and trusted. That sounded nice. Maybe that was why, when Alex put a hesitant arm around her shoulders as he led her away, she found herself leaning into him.

Holly couldn't remember the last time she'd leaned on someone else for support. The realization gave her a moment of anxiety, but she put it firmly aside. There'd be plenty of time to be independent again tomorrow.

Chapter Five

Will was over by the fire truck, talking with Tom. When he saw his mom and his coach coming around the side of the house he went to meet them.

"I'm going to go take Tom home," Alex said to Holly. "It'll only take me a few minutes, then I'll be back for you guys. Wait for me here, okay?"

"Okay," Holly agreed, smiling at him gratefully, and then she was hugging Will, her son who was taller than she was and so wise beyond his years but who would always, at least in her eyes, be her little boy.

"Baby, I'm so sorry."

"Sorry for what?"

Holly laughed through her tears. "For letting our house burn down. You do remember that, don't you? The Stanton home, been in our family for eighty years, now a pile of damp ash? You warned me something was wrong in the kitchen and I didn't pay attention. This is all my fault."

He frowned at her. "You're kidding, right? This is totally *my* fault. I was the one who noticed the smell, but I didn't take it seriously enough to make you come to the kitchen right away to check it out. I let you down. I'm the one who should be sorry."

Holly was staring at him. "Don't do that," she said urgently.

"Do what?"

"Take responsibility for things you're not responsible for."

Will snorted. "Look who's talking. That's your signature move, Mom."

Holly laughed a little shakily. "You're doing that thing where you're so mature it freaks me out."

"Sorry," Will said, with a ghost of his old grin. "I'm sure I'll make up for it later with some stupid teenage behavior."

Mother and son stood for several minutes in silence, watching the firemen at work on the blackened ruin that had once been their home.

After a while Will spoke again. "I've got an idea. How about we agree it was just a terrible accident that's no one's fault?"

Holly took a deep breath and let it out. "Deal," she said, giving him a quick hug. "And by the way, you're freaking me out again."

Alex had come back in time to hear their last exchange.

"You know, I made that exact point earlier, and you punched me in the jaw."

Holly smiled at him. "I guess Will's presentation is just more credible than yours." She reached up a hand

and brushed the hair off Alex's forehead before running her fingers softly across the scar that sliced through his eyebrow to his temple. "I think it's this scar. Gives you a disreputable air."

At the touch of her fingers Alex took in a quick, sharp breath and then went absolutely still, forgetting to breathe at all as he stared down at her. Holly's mind was still full of the events of the evening and she didn't notice the intensity of his reaction.

But someone else did.

Holly was startled when her son smacked himself on the forehead. "What's up, Will?" she asked, turning to look at him.

"Nothing," he said. "Not important. By the way, not that it isn't fun standing around here in front of what used to be a house, but where are we staying tonight? We could probably go to Mrs. Hanneman's if there's nowhere else. Or I guess we could find a hotel. Whatever we're doing, could we do it soon? I feel like I could fall down where I'm standing."

Holly glanced at Alex doubtfully. "Well, your coach suggested we could stay with him for a few days while we—"

"That's a great idea!" Will said, surprising her with his enthusiasm. "I mean…thanks, Coach. It's really nice of you. We won't be any trouble. Or at least I won't. Of course my mom's kind of a handful…."

"I can handle your mom," Alex said firmly. Will broke into a grin. Holly yawned, and stumbled suddenly, and Will and Alex each grabbed her by an arm. "You know, I think I'm a little tired, too," she said, as if surprised by the discovery.

"Okay, time to go," Alex said. "The firemen said we

could leave whenever we wanted, and I told them where you'll be if they need to reach you. My car's across the street. Walking wounded carry the stretcher cases."

Holly drifted in and out of awareness as Alex drove away from her neighborhood near the center of town and out toward the rolling farmlands on the outskirts. The next thing she knew Alex was leading her and Will into a lovely old farmhouse and turning the light on in the front hallway. She looked around her without seeing very much.

"I have three guest bedrooms," Alex was saying as he led them upstairs, "so at least there's plenty of room. There's furniture, too, because I bought this place in an estate sale and a lot of the original stuff stayed." He paused at an open doorway. "Will, why don't you take this room? I'll go find you some towels and a tooth-brush, and you can borrow a pair of my pajamas. Wait right here."

Holly was sorry when Alex disappeared, because his voice had been comforting, a warm, low baritone that somehow made it seem as if everything was going to be all right. She and Will looked around the small bedroom, which was a little bare, with a wrought-iron bedstead and a big oak dresser and not much else. But the bed looked comfortable, and the antique quilt on it was lovely, and Holly felt content to think of her son sleeping here tonight.

After a minute Alex was back with an armful of things for Will, which he set down on the bed. "Do you need anything else?" he asked. "Something to drink?"

Will shook his head. "Mrs. Hanneman gave me water at her place. I'm fine. I think I'm just going to shower and go to bed, if that's okay."

"Of course it's okay. You're not going to school tomorrow, so sleep in as late as you want."

"Hey," Holly protested. "We Stantons are tough. A little thing like the total destruction of everything we own doesn't stop us from going to school and work on Monday morning."

Alex ignored her. "Wake up when you wake up," he said to the teenager, who nodded gratefully.

"Good night, Mom. Good night, Coach," he said, stifling a yawn.

"Good night, Will," Alex said, steering Holly out of the room.

"Well, I guess it's all right for Will to take a day off," Holly grumbled, "but not me. You got that, Alex McKenna?" she asked as he led her down the hall and into another bedroom. "I am going to get up at 7:00 a.m. like I always do and will you *look* at that *bed!*" she exclaimed when she saw it, a beautiful queen-size four-poster, with a scalloped headboard and a crocheted canopy.

"I thought you might like it," said Alex, sounding pleased.

"It's gorgeous," Holly said, running a caressing hand over the carving on one of the bedposts. "I always wanted a bed like this, but I couldn't justify spending the money."

"Well," Alex said. "I aim to please. You even have your very own bathroom, right through that door. I'll go get you some towels and things."

Alex disappeared and Holly wandered over to check out the bathroom. It was painted white and looked reasonably clean, if a little dilapidated. The bathtub, on the other hand, was absolutely incredible. A real Victorian style claw-foot tub that looked big enough to swim laps in.

Alex found her in the bathroom when he returned.

"What do you think?" he asked as he hung fresh towels over the bar behind the door and took a new toothbrush out of its box, placing it carefully in the holder on the sink.

"I would really love to take a bath in that thing," Holly said, gazing wistfully at the tub.

"Well, then, why don't you?"

Holly sighed. "It just seems too complicated right now. I'm so tired, Alex… I've never been this exhausted in my entire life. I think I'll just go to bed and take a bath in the morning."

He looked at her with one eyebrow up. "No offense, Holly, but you reek of smoke, and you look like a war refugee with all the dried blood. Don't you think you might sleep better if you were clean? Especially when you add in the health factor of washing those scratches and getting antiseptic on them."

Holly made a face. "You run me a bath then, since you're so picky." She rested her back against the bathroom wall and slid slowly down until she came to a sitting position. "I'll just wait here so I don't get your furniture all dirty."

Alex looked down at her for a moment. She looked small and forlorn in her dirty nightgown with her red hair wild around her pale smudged face, and she still had more attitude in her little finger than any woman he'd ever met. "Fine," he said, shaking his head.

This was all he needed, he thought, as he turned on the water and it thundered into the tub in a cloud of steam. It was bad enough she'd be sleeping under his roof, now he was running her a bath she'd be getting into soon, where she'd be naked and wet and…

"There's no soap in here," he said, not looking at Holly. "Just let the tub fill while I get some."

When he came back Holly's head was resting against the wall and her eyes were closed. Alex checked the water level, turning off the faucet and testing the temperature with his hand. Hot but not too hot. Nice and deep, too. This tub was huge.

A worrisome thought occurred and he asked, "You're not going to fall asleep in there, are you? It would be pretty pathetic if you escaped a fire only to drown in my bathtub."

Holly opened her eyes and shook her head solemnly. "Nope, I won't drown. At least I don't think I will. Thank you for running the bath, Alex." She sat there, blinking up at him, and Alex held out a hand to pull her to her feet.

"Tell you what," he said reluctantly. "You get in there and have a good soak, and I'll go get some antiseptic and something for you to wear to bed, and then I'll wait outside to make sure you're okay."

"That would be nice," Holly said seriously.

She reached for the buttons on her nightgown and Alex backed away hastily. "Okay, then, I'll be in the bedroom. Take your time, have fun, don't fall asleep." He got out of there fast and closed the door behind him, breathing a sigh of relief.

Oh, boy, was this a bad idea, he thought to himself as he looked in his dresser for something to give Holly to wear. How long was she going to be here? Long enough to drive him insane with lust? Could lust actually drive a person insane? Maybe he'd be the first American male to test that theory. The first one committed to an institution after a week of living under the same roof with a woman he couldn't have.

You asked for this, Alex thought grimly as he

grabbed hydrogen peroxide and bandages from his medicine chest. He'd invited them to stay here. Both of them, he reminded himself. Let's not forget the fifteen-year-old kid in the next bedroom. Even if Holly could be persuaded to sleep with him, which would never happen for about a hundred different reasons, the most important was that her son was staying here, too.

Alex sat down on her bed to wait for Holly to finish, and a few minutes later she opened the door.

"Hi," she said, blushing a little and keeping a tight grip on the front of her towel. She looked a little more awake now, her face pink, her hair lying in damp red ringlets against her bare shoulders, with droplets of water still clinging to her skin.

Alex levered himself up and started to retreat toward the door. "The medicine and bandages are on the bed. I brought you some things you could sleep in, too. I wasn't sure what would be the most comfortable, so I brought you a couple of different pajama tops and some T-shirts. No, um, underwear of course—" he coughed "—but there'll be plenty of time to go shopping tomorrow. I'll take you in the morning, when you wake up."

She was frowning at him. "I'm going to work in the morning."

At least when she was irritating it helped distract him from her body. "No, you're not," he said, speaking slowly and distinctly.

"Yes, I am," she said, speaking just as slowly and distinctly.

Alex sighed and tried to think of her weaknesses. "You're just going to leave Will to cope with the trauma by himself?" Holly bit her lip and he pursued his advantage. "All I'm suggesting is that you take one day off to spend time with your son, so both of you can recover a little. Besides," he added reasonably, "you don't have anything to wear to work, unless you want to go in a pair of my pajamas. We need to take you shopping for one of those boring suits you like before you can go back."

She was glaring at him, but he could tell he had her. "Fine," she said grudgingly. "I will take one day off." Her glare suddenly gave way to an enormous yawn. "I guess I should go to bed now," she said, looking and sounding exhausted, and Alex nodded.

"Good night, Holly," he said at the door.

"Good night, Alex."

He closed the door softly behind him and went down the hall to his own bed, where he lay awake a long time before he finally fell asleep.

Holly woke up sore and aching and with a weary lassitude in every muscle. She opened her eyes, and memories of last night came flooding back.

There was a sudden weight in her chest, a clogging in her throat, a stinging behind her eyes. She turned her head into the pillow and cried for her home, for everything that had been lost. She cried for a long time.

After a while the tears stopped coming, and she rolled onto her back again. She lay there for several minutes, taking in deep breaths and letting them out again, watching the play of sunlight on the blue-and-green quilt. She turned her head to look out of the window and saw a huge maple tree right outside, glorious in October shades of red and orange and yellow.

There was a knock on her door, and when she called out, "Come in," Alex was there.

He looked easy and comfortable in sweatpants and an old T-shirt. He had a pair of jeans over his arm, and he was carrying a tray.

"I must have done something right in a past life, after all," she said, sitting up against the headboard. "At least men keep bringing me breakfast in bed."

"Men?" Alex repeated with a frown, setting the tray down over her knees and sitting down on the foot of the bed. "What men? Who's been bringing you breakfast in bed?"

"Just Will," she answered, inhaling the delicious aroma of coffee and hot buttered toast. There was fruit, too, sliced up and arranged on a plate. "He's on this health kick, thanks to you I think, where he insists on cooking us both a lot of hearty breakfasts that I never eat." She looked again at the tray in front of her. "Normally I don't have a big appetite when I first wake up in the morning, but this really looks good."

Holly glanced up in time to catch his grin, and her heart skipped a beat. That was one killer smile. And now she'd be seeing it every day.

"That's because it isn't morning," he informed her. "It's two o'clock in the afternoon. You slept for twelve hours, beating your son by about forty-five minutes. He's had his hearty breakfast and is now downstairs pawing through my music collection. What does it mean when a fifteen-year-old likes your taste in CDs? Does it mean you're really cool, or that he's kind of a geek?"

"Will is not a geek," she said indignantly.

"Which must mean I'm cool," he said smugly, grinning at her again, which made her think it might be a good idea to focus on something else, like her coffee.

She looked down at the big blue mug, three quarters full of steaming black fluid, and added cream and sugar with careful attention.

"Mmm," she said after the first sip and looked at him in surprise. "You make good coffee."

"After thirty-five years as a bachelor, yes, I have learned to make good coffee."

He was looking at the left side of her face as he spoke, and suddenly he leaned forward, running the tip of his index finger lightly over the scratch there. It hadn't turned out to be very deep or serious after Holly had cleaned it last night, and she hadn't even bothered with a Band-Aid.

The sensation of Alex's fingertip tickled a little bit, making her shiver, and Holly turned her head away. But then his fingers were twining around a strand of her hair that he tucked behind her ear. Holly drew in a sharp breath.

"That scratch looks a lot better today," he said softly, his touch lingering, and Holly felt her stomach muscles tighten. She licked her lips nervously and Alex pulled away, clearing his throat.

"Unfortunately, I don't make much else other than coffee, although I do manage to eat a lot of fruits and vegetables and reasonably healthy things. I'm just not very creative in the kitchen."

"Not interested in the culinary arts?" Holly asked, pleased that her voice sounded so normal.

Alex shrugged. "There doesn't seem to be much point when you live alone. Maybe now that you and Will are here I'll get inspired. I'll have to get some more interesting groceries, though. Speaking of shopping, I thought we could hit the mall today to buy you and Will some clothes and other necessaries. I know we're not going to be able to replace everything you lost overnight, but at least we can make a start."

Holly was staring at him. "You're a good guy," she said slowly, as if realizing it for the first time. "You really are a good guy. You're not a jerk." She shook her head. "I was wrong about you, Alex."

Alex raised an eyebrow. "Well, thanks. It's good that you don't think I'm a jerk anymore. Let me return the compliment. You're a good guy, too, Holly Stanton."

Holly started to smile. He looked so cute sitting there at the foot of the bed, his brown hair a little tousled and his blue eyes crinkling up at the corners when he smiled at her like that. She really *liked* him. How could she have missed out on a potential friendship like this?

"Nope," she said now, enjoying herself. "Not good enough. I'm going to make you refute every one of the lousy things you've said to me over the years. Uptight, for instance."

He considered it. "Well, you look pretty relaxed right now, so I guess I can take that one back."

"Stuck up and holier-than-thou."

"Okay, that I don't even have to think about. Definitely not."

"Stubborn."

Alex snorted. "Sorry, kid, but that one I'm going to stand by."

Holly made a face at him. "Fine. What else did you call me? Oh, right. Repressed."

Alex's eyebrows went up and he grinned again, this time slow and lazy, and Holly felt a sudden blaze of heat that started down low and moved through all her limbs. "Well," he drawled. "Let me see. I think you blew that one out of water on Saturday night, wouldn't you say?"

It was her own fault for bringing it up, Holly thought, blushing furiously. She'd been hoping to avoid any references to Saturday night as long as she was staying in Alex's house, and here she'd gone and reminded him of it.

She suddenly remembered that she was wearing one of Alex's T-shirts and no underwear. The shirt was huge on her, but it had ridden up above her hips, and right at the moment the blanket didn't seem like very much protection….

She forced herself to meet Alex's eyes, trying to think of some way to change the subject, when he leaned forward a little. "Did anyone ever tell you you're absolutely adorable when you blush like that?"

Now the blush went from head to toe, and Holly had a sneaking suspicion he knew it.

"Darn you, Alex, you did that on purpose. Now I can't stop." She pressed her hands against her hot cheeks. "Cut it out."

He leaned closer, tracing her bottom lip with a fingertip until she shivered.

"Cut what out?" he asked, his voice innocent.

She had to do something to stop this. Her pulse was racing and her breath was trapped somewhere in her throat and her body was on fire, and Alex could not be allowed to know how he made her feel, or at least not the full extent of it, because the humiliation of that would force her to leave, and this was a really comfortable bed and the bathtub was out of this world. Not to mention it would put an end to the friendship that had just begun between her and Alex and which already seemed too important to jeopardize.

She took a deep breath. *"That,"* she said firmly,

pushing his hand away and getting a grip on her self-possession. "I watched you flirt your way through high school and I know it comes naturally to you, but it doesn't to me and I don't appreciate it. You're just going to have to learn how to interact with a woman without flirting. It'll be good for you."

She frowned at him in sudden seriousness. "I really want this friendship thing to work, Alex. Will likes you, and *I* like you, which is a new thing and a little weird but nice, and we're staying in your house. Please don't ruin it by flirting with me. I know it doesn't mean anything to you, I know it's just how you are with women, but…well, I don't like it. Let's not mess this up, okay?"

Alex had pulled back, and Holly waited for his reaction. She'd told him the truth—at least most of it—and if he couldn't deal with it, it was better she find out now.

"Mess this up," he said finally, taking a deep breath. "No. That's the last thing I want, too. It really is. I'm sorry, Holly," he said almost formally, and Holly bit her lip, glad he was okay with what she'd said but wishing she could bring back the easy camaraderie they'd been sharing earlier.

Oh, well, she told herself, it would come back. And it would have gone up in flames if she hadn't stopped what was happening before. If Alex had gone on touching her like that, there was a good chance she would have jumped him, and that would have screwed her life up in ways she didn't like to think about. For one thing she would have been scraping her ego off the floor after Alex tried to explain he'd just been flirting, you know, like he always did, and he was sorry but he wasn't really interested in her that way and besides her son was right downstairs and my God, did she have no moral fortitude at all?

Yes, I do, she thought firmly, as Alex slid off the bed.

"Take all the time you want getting up. I borrowed the jeans from a neighbor, who's a little bigger than you, but they should get you through the day. As soon as you're ready we'll go shopping."

"Sounds good," she said, and Alex smiled at her briefly before making an exit.

Holly stared at the door he closed behind him, trying not to miss the heat she'd felt just a moment ago.

Chapter Six

Stupid, stupid, stupid. He was a grown man, not some hormone-driven kid.

And yet Alex literally couldn't keep his hands off of Holly Stanton. When he was with her, he wanted to touch her. It was like a compulsion. Of course it didn't help seeing her in bed, all sleepy and tousled and wearing one of his T-shirts, but still, he'd only lasted five minutes before reaching out to caress that perfect lower lip. In the next moment he would have put his mouth on hers, hot and hard, and the image was so appealing and so terrifying he was having trouble thinking about anything else.

God, he was such a jerk. Here was a woman who'd just lost her home in a fire, who was a guest in his house, and he'd started to make a move on her.

At least she'd thought it was just "how he was with women." A little casual flirting on his part.

Alex paused in the upper hallway and leaned on the banister. Thankfully she didn't know it was anything *but* casual. That no woman had ever affected him the way Holly did.

It was ironic, really. Alex had been with a lot of women, and had fun with most of them. He hoped that most of them had had fun, too. But none of those relationships had ever seemed to matter very much. They were enjoyable while they lasted, and that was it. He never felt as if he was necessary in any woman's life, and no woman had ever been necessary to him.

Then there was Holly. Almost from the moment they'd met, he'd felt a connection to her. It was as if he had X-ray vision where Holly was concerned, letting him see the passion and vulnerability she hid from the world. Things no one else seemed to care about. And because he could see her so clearly, he'd always felt as if she needed him. Needed him in a way no other woman ever had.

And that was the true irony. She needed him, and he failed her—time after time.

He'd never been able to help her. He hadn't talked her out of dating Brian; he hadn't convinced her to marry him when she was pregnant and alone. Hell, she hadn't even let him change her flat tire.

Last night was the first time Holly Stanton had accepted any kind of help from him.

And here he was, ready to ruin it. Ready to act on an attraction she didn't share and didn't need to deal with right now—and to jeopardize a friendship that was less than twenty-four hours old.

Maybe the connection he felt to Holly was always meant to be a friendship. Maybe his desire for her had gotten in the way of that—even when they were teenagers. Especially when they were teenagers.

Maybe that was why he'd always failed her.

Well, he wasn't going to fail this time.

Alex sighed and headed downstairs for the living room, deciding to see what Will was up to. With Will, at least things were straightforward. Football. Music. The basics.

Will was literally surrounded with music right now, half of Alex's CD collection in little piles on the living room floor. "I'm reorganizing them for you," he explained.

Alex sat on the floor with his back against his overstuffed sofa.

"We're going to create categories. Not too many, because then it gets confusing and harder to maintain. Just the biggies. So far I've got classic rock, rhythm and blues, punk, metal, modern rock and jazz. We'll be alphabetizing within the categories, of course. Anything that doesn't fit we'll call eclectic and put at the end."

Alex put his hands behind his head and leaned back comfortably against his couch, thinking about how much he liked kids in general and this kid in particular. "You're more like your mom than I thought. This is not a compliment, by the way."

Will grinned at him. "Sure it is. And a little organization won't kill you. Especially considering all this great raw material," he added.

"Does Holly like music?" Alex couldn't help asking.

"Yeah, she does. Actually, my mom's taste in music isn't too terrible, considering."

"Considering her advanced age, you mean?"

"Exactly. It tends more toward the classic rock end, but at least within her limits she has good taste."

Alex started to get interested. "Like what? Give me some examples."

Will thought about it. "Well, Bruce Springsteen's big. 'Thunder Road' and 'Born to Run' are two of her favorite songs. Then there's Van Morrison. 'Moondance' and 'Crazy Love.' Joni Mitchell's 'Blue,' the entire album. Everything Aretha Franklin ever did."

Alex sat up straighter. "Keep going. What else?"

"How come you're so interested in my mom's taste in music?" Will asked.

"Well, I'm interested in your mom. I mean," he added hastily, "I'm interested in being friends with your mom. Considering we're going to be under the same roof for a while, it's probably a good idea for me to learn more about her. And music, important music—the kind you'd bring with you to a desert island—is like a map of a person's soul."

Will was still studying him, and Alex felt a little uncomfortable. But after a minute he started talking again.

"She likes a lot of eighties stuff." Will shook his head. "She has this secret passion for Joan Jett, which she thinks I don't know about. She has…well, she used to have…a couple of albums by Foreigner, and one by Air Supply." He shuddered in mock horror at that, but Alex had been distracted by something else. The change in verb tense.

"Wow, kid," he said slowly. "It's just starting to hit me. You really lost everything last night. All your books, all your music."

Will made a wry face. "Yeah. The books don't bother me much but the music's pretty hard to take. Although from what I see here, I'll be able to recreate a lot of my collection by copying yours. A lot of my mom's favorites are in here, too. She's a big Rolling Stones fan."

"No kidding," Alex said, surprised.

"Why is the floor covered in CDs?" Holly asked. They turned to see her coming down the stairs.

"We're talking about music," Will said. "Coach was asking what you like. He says a person's taste in music is like a map of their soul."

Holly looked at him with an eyebrow raised.

Alex shrugged. "Okay, so I waxed poetic. Even football coaches are allowed to do that once in a while."

"Sure," Holly said skeptically, sitting down in an armchair next to the couch. "Okay, then, what does my musical taste tell you about me? Assuming Will actually knows what my musical taste is."

"Well," Alex said, leaning back again. "Some of it, we'll hope, is not significant. Like Foreigner. But there seems to be a clear pattern in some of the other stuff. Joan Jett, Bruce Springsteen—that's the rebel touch. Bad girls and bad boys. The Stones even more so. But there's also passion and intensity, hunger for life. 'Thunder Road' and 'Born to Run' are about busting out, breaking free."

Holly frowned. "Hey, I just like those songs. I don't have a secret urge to rebel."

Alex ignored her. "Van Morrison and Joni Mitchell are all about love. Love that changes you forever, love that burns you up and heals you at the same time. The kind of love you can't live without."

He glanced at Holly and saw surprise in her eyes. She probably didn't think he was capable of using the word love in a sentence. He grinned at her. "Aretha Franklin, on the other hand, is just a woman with the greatest voice God ever bestowed on a human being. You don't need any other reasons for Aretha. We'll just put her down to good taste."

Will was grinning, too. "No deep psychological analysis?"

"Nope." He rose to his feet and reached out a hand to help Holly up. "So, who's ready to go shopping?"

At one point during their mall trip they split up, Holly trying on clothes while Will and Alex went to two different music stores. As a surprise for Holly, Alex bought every CD of hers that Will could name. They had a great time, talking about bands and musicians and concerts they had seen and would like to see. And Will had come up with a list of his mom's all-time favorite songs, or at least as many as he could remember, and Alex had written them all down.

Later that night, after Holly and Will went to bed, he used the list to make Holly a mix CD.

It was a little like being with her, Alex thought as he burned the last song and let it roll over him as he sat back on the couch. The song was Marvin Gaye's "Let's Get It On," which was one he'd already had on hand and which happened to be one of his all-time favorites, as well.

He grinned suddenly as he realized he was acting like a lovestruck college student, making a mix tape for his latest crush. Well, at least he'd moved on from high school. He was progressing. By next week maybe he'd be up to his late twenties.

Man, this was a sexy song. Alex closed his eyes and imagined kissing Holly to this song, swaying with her on a dance floor somewhere and feeling every inch of her pressed against him as he tasted her, slow and soft at first and then hard and insistent, bringing out the passion he knew was just under the surface, waiting to be unleashed.

Alex sighed and pressed a cushion to his face. Yeah, he had it bad.

He headed upstairs for bed, pausing as he walked past Holly's door to lay a palm flat against the wood, thinking of her on the other side, curled up in bed with her red hair fanned out across the pillow.

Then he heard her call out his name.

He froze.

"Alex," he heard again, distinctly, and there was no question it was Holly's voice.

Okay, this was weird. Did she know he was out here? How could she? Was something wrong? Did she need him?

Confused, uncertain, Alex turned the knob as softly as he could and slipped inside her room, his eyes adjusting to the darkness and moonlight as he focused on the figure curled up on the bed.

"Holly?" he asked softly, barely above a whisper. "Is everything all right? Do you need something?"

She didn't answer him. After a moment or two of listening to her deep, even breathing, Alex decided that she was definitely asleep and that his mind had been playing tricks on him. Time to make his getaway before she woke up and punched him again, this time with cause.

He'd put his hand on the door knob when she stirred, stretching languidly.

"Alex," she said clearly.

She was still asleep. She was lying in full moonlight now and he could see that her eyes were closed. What the—

And then she said it again, softly.

"Alex…"

There was warmth in her voice and a kind of longing.

"Alex," she said a third time, a sensual whisper that went straight to his groin. She shifted a little in her sleep.

For one unbearable minute Alex just stood there. Then he turned the knob soundlessly and got the hell out, shutting her door softly and firmly behind him and moving swiftly down the hall.

Alex ran a shaking hand across his forehead. This was bad. Oh, man, this was bad. It had been torture enough just imagining what her voice would sound like saying his name like that. Now he knew, and the reality was more intense than his fantasies, and Alex couldn't think of the last time that had happened.

He'd courted the torture. Hell, he'd sent an engraved invitation. If he hadn't been standing outside her door like some kind of lovesick puppy dog he never would have heard her. He wasn't *supposed* to have heard her. He'd been listening in to her dreams, and if torture was the result, well, it was his own fault.

Maybe he should be glad that at least he knew, now, that she felt some of what he did. But somehow it made it worse, knowing that her subconscious or unconscious or whatever felt something for him, while her conscious had made it perfectly clear she didn't even want him to flirt with her.

And now the image of her moving in her sleep, her back arching ever so slightly and her lips parting, was burned into his brain.

But no matter what sleeping Holly thought about him, wide-awake Holly had asked him to keep his distance, in very clear and unambiguous terms. And somehow, someway, he was going to find a way to manage it.

Starting tomorrow, he was going to spend every waking hour focused on football and his players. And if that didn't work, maybe he could pack himself in ice.

That ought to do it.

Holly woke up slowly, feeling a delicious warmth running through her body. She stretched, thoroughly and with pleasure, feeling how delightful it was to move, to use her muscles. She must have gotten a really good night's sleep, she decided.

Then her dream came flooding back. Alex. She'd dreamed about Alex last night.

She'd fantasized plenty, but she'd never had an honest to goodness dream about him. Or any man. Not like that, anyway. Come to think of it, this was the first sexy dream she'd ever had in her life.

It had been so real. Alex above her, Alex inside her, Alex surrounding her. It had been so real that the sexual languor started to wear off and embarrassment took its place.

Which was ridiculous, of course. She had no control over her dreams. And she was attracted to Alex, even though she had no plans of ever telling *him* that, so it wasn't all that surprising that he'd pop up in her subconscious now and again.

Holly glanced at the clock. She'd gone to bed early so she'd be able to wake up early, and it had worked. It was six-thirty in the morning; she'd beaten the alarm by half an hour. She could get up, shower, dress, have breakfast with Will and still be at work by eight.

The only problem was, she didn't want to move. She wanted to lie here with her eyes closed and imagine Alex touching her.

Suddenly disgusted with herself, Holly threw off the covers and slid her legs out to the floor. The weather had turned cooler last night and the floorboards were cold against her bare feet, sending a good bracing shiver through her as she headed for the bathroom. She added a good bracing shower, followed by a careful application of minimal, professional makeup. She picked out the most sober of all the outfits she'd bought yesterday, a dark gray wool pantsuit with a subdued pinstripe of lighter gray. Under it she wore a utilitarian bra and a gray cashmere turtleneck. Add to that her trusty chignon and a pair of low heels and she was ready to face the world.

Her head high and her steps brisk, she headed downstairs to see if Will was up before her. Alex would probably still be asleep, since his day started late and ended late.

Only he wasn't asleep. He was right there in the kitchen when she came around the corner, and she actually crashed into him before she could stop herself.

He jumped away from her like he'd been shot.

"Holly!" he said, backing up to the other end of the kitchen. She must really have startled him.

And then, just as she'd feared, the sight of him brought back her dream in living color and she felt herself blushing. "Um, is Will up yet?" she asked to cover.

"Yes, he's—"

"Here I am, Mom. Wow, you're up early! I told Coach you wouldn't be awake until twenty minutes before you had to leave for work."

"Right. Well, I wanted to get an early start. You, too, I see. And you, Alex."

"I'm on my way out the door now," he said quickly. "And I'll be back pretty late tonight. Go ahead and have dinner without me. I've got a lot of administrative chores to take care of, and then there's the Steeltown game to prepare for. I'll see you at practice, Will." He started to head for the back door.

"Hey, Coach!" Will called out.

"What?" Alex answered over his shoulder, sounding impatient.

"Aren't you forgetting something?" he asked significantly, indicating his mother.

Alex looked back at her, nonplussed. "Oh. Right." He paused a moment, frowning, and then backtracked for the living room.

"What's going on?" Holly asked Will.

"You'll see," he said.

Alex came back carrying a gaily if inexpertly wrapped package.

"Here," he said without much ceremony, plunking it down on the kitchen table in front of Holly. "Something for you that Will and I picked up yesterday."

Holly had forgotten the present that the two of them had hidden from her. She ripped open the bright paper and gasped when she saw all the CDs that spilled out.

"These are all... How did you..." She got it suddenly and smiled at her son. "You told him what to get." She turned the smile on Alex. "And you spent way, way too much money on these. I should be mad, but...this really helps," she said. "I mean, I know we're not going to re-create everything we had, but this—well, this helps a lot. Thank you."

"Anytime," Alex said. "I mean it, Holly. You and Will lost so much, and it's going to take a long time to put it all back together again, but if I can do anything to help, you only have to ask."

She smiled at him a little crookedly, and he smiled back at her, the warmth she'd begun to rely on lighting up his blue eyes.

"Have dinner without me tonight," he said again, heading to the back door. "See you later, Will. I hope you have a good day back at work, Holly."

"Thanks," she answered, but he was out the door and she didn't think he'd heard her.

A little odd, but very sweet, was Alex McKenna. If someone had told her seventy-two hours ago that's how she'd be characterizing him today, she would have laughed at them.

A few minutes later Holly was sliding one of her new CDs into the car stereo and backing out of Alex's driveway.

She'd picked one at random and it turned out to be Van Morrison, an album she hadn't listened to in a while. The music tugged at her, and she remembered the conversation yesterday between Alex and Will. About music being a map of your soul.

She braked at a stoplight and her fingers drummed against the steering wheel. She wasn't sure she wanted anyone running around with a map of her soul. Definitely not Alex.

Just as she was thinking that the light turned green and the next song began. It was "Moondance," and in the blink of an eye Holly was engulfed in an old memory.

It was prom night, and Brian, now a freshman in college, had come home to be her escort. They were still boyfriend and girlfriend, and Holly was sure she loved him, although he seemed even busier and more ambitious now that he was actually taking the pre-law classes he'd dreamed about.

Still, he had taken the time to come home for her prom. Holly appreciated the gesture even though they didn't really have a good time. Not a bad time exactly, just not a good time. Neither of them was big on dancing. Brian would never engage in anything so frivolous, and Holly was too shy to dance in public, although she loved to bop around in her room at home.

They decided to leave early. Brian went to say his goodbyes and get their coats, while Holly went to get one more glass of punch.

She was waiting for Brian at the edge of the dance floor, gazing wistfully at all the couples—the band had just started to play Van Morrison's "Moondance," which was one of her favorite songs—when someone came up behind her and slid his arms around her waist.

She could tell it wasn't Brian. There was something a little too…well, *physical*…in the way those arms felt against her, in the way those hands moved slowly over her hips.

"Want to dance?" a voice said softly in her ear, and Holly twisted around to see Alex McKenna standing there, his face only inches from hers, his blue eyes glinting with mischief and something else.

Holly pulled away sharply, angry at the way her body had responded before she'd known it was him.

She had caught glimpses of Alex all evening, dancing with a dozen different girls—bad girls mostly, including her friend Brenda, but a few good girls, too—all of whom had seemed only too happy to be in his company.

Holly had noticed the contrast between his partners

and herself. Her dress had a high collar and big puffy sleeves, and the white satin material made it look a little like a wedding gown. The girls Alex favored tended to wear red or black, cut low in the front or the back or both, with spaghetti straps or no straps at all. Some of them had come here with dates, some alone, but all of them seemed more interested in Alex than any other guy in the room.

Alex had come stag, of course. He wasn't exactly the boyfriend or prom date type. Truth be told, Holly had been surprised to see him here at all, and in a tux no less.

Of course he didn't look like any of the other boys, despite being dressed exactly the same. He had none of the stiff, awkward formality that made them look like kids playing dress up. In fact, he looked oddly debonair, with his bleached blond hair looking natural for once instead of spiked up, and wearing his tux easily, comfortably, as if he'd been born in it.

"I know you want to dance," he said now, his eyes challenging her to deny it. "I've been watching you move your hips to the music while stick-in-the-mud Brian lectures about life."

His eyes were bright as he stepped close to her. "Just one dance, Holly," he said seductively, his mouth near enough that she got a whiff of his breath.

"You're *drunk,*" she said accusingly, taking a step back.

He grinned at her wickedly. "Maybe a little," he admitted.

She glared at him suspiciously. "You didn't spike the punch, did you? Because if you did—"

"You'll tell on me? Don't worry, Holly, you don't need to get your panties in a twist. I didn't spike the punch." He reached into a pocket and pulled out a small silver flask. "See? Just for me. You and your boring friends don't have to worry."

"My friends are *not* boring."

Alex slipped the flask back in his pocket. "Well, maybe not as boring as your date. Where is the college boy, by the way?"

"He's getting our coats," she said stiffly. "We're going home."

"Right." Alex pulled back a little. "Heading out to do the nasty, I suppose," he said, his voice unconcerned.

"Of course not," Holly snapped. "God, Alex, why do you always have to be so crude?"

He stared at her. "You're leaving your prom early and it's not to have sex?"

"That's right," Holly said coldly. "Brian respects me."

"He respects you," Alex repeated. He shook his head slowly. "What I'm thinking right now can't be true. It's too pathetic even for Brian. But is it possible he's been dating you for two years and never in all that time made a move?"

Holly glared at him. "Of course he's made a move. Brian's a fantastic kisser." Actually that wasn't the case, but she'd be damned if she'd let Alex know it.

"A fantastic kisser. Right. I'm not talking about kissing, Holly. Have. You. Had. Sex."

"Of course not!" Holly said, outraged that he'd asked her that and outraged that she was even standing here having this conversation. "What kind of girl do you think I am?"

Alex took two quick steps and grabbed her by the shoulders, looking at her with unexpected intensity in his blue eyes.

"A girl who deserves to be with a guy who appreciates what he's got. If you were mine, Holly, I'd seduce you every night of your life. I'd throw you on the back of my bike and take you somewhere private, somewhere I could find out what's underneath all this."

His eyes roved downward, and in spite of her high collar and puffy sleeves Holly felt exposed under his gaze, vulnerable. His hands moved to her waist, and she had been so slender back then that his thumbs and fingers had almost met as they circled her. She had never realized how big and powerful his hands were, and yet his touch was unexpectedly gentle.

She had never felt so fragile and feminine. Brian's hands were much smaller.

His eyes met hers again. They were so blue, so penetrating, and they seemed to see things other people didn't. Things that no one should see. When he spoke his voice was low, and rough with some quality she couldn't name.

"Brian doesn't seem very curious about what's inside this package, but I am. Why are you with him, Holly? Why do you hide behind all this?" Somehow she guessed he wasn't just talking about her prom dress.

His hands were still on her waist, but now they moved up her torso, slowly, until his thumbs just brushed the underside of her breasts.

She'd never felt like this before. There was a strange, hollow feeling in all of her bones. She closed her eyes, unable to move, and when Alex spoke again his voice was right by her ear.

"You don't belong with him," he whispered.

She was standing on the edge of an abyss. One step and she'd go over.

Her eyes flew open. "I *hate* you," she spat at him, finally finding her voice. She shoved him away from her and looked desperately around for Brian, furious at herself for the melting heat she'd felt at his words, for the goose bumps he'd raised with his touch and most of all for how long it had taken her to push him away.

Alex backed off. "Maybe you hate me, but at least I'm *alive*," he said nastily. "Near as I can tell, Brian's ready for the undertaker. And you? Let's see, what's the word I'm looking for? Starts with F and rhymes with rigid—"

Brian finally made his appearance, saving Holly from making a scene at her own prom by punching Alex in the face. She'd grabbed Brian by the arm and stormed away, refusing to look back at Alex and unable to speak until she'd had a few minutes to cool down.

But that hadn't been the end of that memorable evening. With Alex's words and Alex's taunting expression playing over and over in her head, Holly had practically attacked Brian in the front seat of his car.

Abruptly, Holly came back to the present.

Oh, well, at least she could laugh about it now. Sort of. And one good thing had come out of that night. A great thing, actually. Will.

Holly sighed as she pulled into the company parking lot. Alex had always had the ability to get under her skin, whether he was making her furious or making her hot. The night of the prom…yesterday in her bedroom…last night's dream.

At least she didn't have to worry about him flirting with her anymore. Ever since she'd asked him to stop doing that with her, he'd gone along with her request. She'd asked for friendship and that's what she was getting.

And Alex's friendship was a gift she should be grateful for. He was generous and kind, and he made her laugh, and Will was crazy about him. That was what she wanted. A good, safe friendship. Not the other stuff. The dangerous, pulse-accelerating, nitroglycerin stuff.

Yes, Alex was giving her what she wanted. Trying to not feel depressed at that knowledge and resolving to put Alex firmly out of her mind for the next eight hours, Holly stepped out of her car and prepared to once again take the world of financial planning by storm.

Chapter Seven

Well, it was working. Sort of. Alex supposed he should consider himself lucky that Steeltown was going to present such a challenge Friday night. Preparing for the game kept him from thinking about Holly every five minutes.

Unfortunately, he didn't feel that lucky. Steeltown was big and mean, and had a reputation for playing dirty. Late hits, personal fouls, all the things no coach liked to think about, especially with a young, light, inexperienced squad.

He worked his kids hard, telling them in no uncertain terms that the team they were about to face, on their turf, was going to be their toughest test yet.

He was proud of them, Alex thought when he'd wrapped things up and sent them to the showers. If guts and hard work could do it, they'd hold their own against Steeltown Friday night.

Now if only he could hold his own against Holly Stanton.

Last night they'd eaten at the mall after their afternoon of shopping. Tonight, Alex stayed resolutely in his office until he figured Will and Holly had finished dinner, trying not to think of how fun it would be to share a meal with them at his big dining room table, the one he hardly ever used since he usually ate off a TV tray in the living room.

It was easy to imagine what it would be like. Mother and son would talk and laugh and include him in all their jokes and affection and warmth. Alex was amazed at how much he wanted that, and then realized he was having a fantasy about Holly that for once had absolutely nothing to do with sex.

Alex sighed and filed the last of his paperwork, grabbing his jacket from the door and turning out the light. He shut and locked his office door and walked along the silent, empty corridor toward the exit.

Sometimes it felt a little strange to be back in this place. It also made the don't-think-about-Holly project tougher, since his memories of high school were all intertwined with memories of Holly. It was good to be back, too, though. It gave him a chance to redeem himself, to make up for the mistakes he'd made as a teenager by helping other kids avoid them.

As hard as it was to live in the same town as Holly Stanton, Alex knew he belonged here, at least for now. He liked this town and he liked the kids he was coaching. He believed in them. They needed him. Well, they needed someone, anyway, and he'd do until someone better came along.

Alex grinned as he pulled into his driveway. Hell, he

even liked his drafty old house. He was almost looking forward to the off-season, when he'd have time to take care of it. By then, maybe Holly and Will would be gone and he could get his sanity back, too.

Alex walked through the front door and knew immediately that something was different. He turned on the light and looked around.

The place was *clean.* Someone had vacuumed, and dusted and done something that made the whole place smell fresh and crisp and lemony.

"Alex, is that you?" Holly called out as she came out of the kitchen, wearing jeans and his Pittsburgh Steelers T-shirt. He was going to let her keep it, because to ever wear it himself after it had been on her, drenched in her warmth and her scent, was not going to be possible. She was holding some kind of cleanser in one hand and she looked guilty.

"What did you do?" he asked suspiciously.

She looked guiltier. "I'm sorry, Alex. I didn't mean to do the whole stereotype. You know, waltz into the bachelor's house and wield domestic tyranny. It's just I don't think you've dusted since, well, forever, and I didn't want Will developing asthma or anything. Especially now that I'm counting on him to get a football scholarship, join the NFL and buy me a yacht."

Alex folded his arms. "I have so dusted."

She raised an eyebrow. "There are dust bunnies in this house that could do battle with Godzilla."

"I've never seen any dust bunnies," he said.

"That's because they were under the couch and behind furniture, places I don't think you visit very often."

"Well, there you go. I mean, who cleans under stuff and behind stuff? That's just a little too anal-retentive for me. I'm a free and easy kind of guy," he added, a grin breaking through his mock-defensiveness. Truthfully, it was fun to come home to a house that looked and smelled this good, especially when he hadn't had to do any of the work. Not that he'd mind doing the work if this was how Holly liked things.

"I would've done this if you'd asked," he told her. "You're a guest. You shouldn't have to clean."

"Oh, I didn't mind. I like to keep busy." She turned back toward the kitchen. "There's leftover chicken casserole if you want some," she said over her shoulder, and Alex followed behind her like a homing pigeon, telling himself it was because he was hungry even though he'd had a huge sandwich at the deli on his way home.

"Mmm, smells good," he said, looking around in amazement at his now sparkling-clean kitchen. "Wow, Holly. This must have taken hours."

"Not really," she said, scooping some casserole onto a plate and handing it to him. "And like I said, I was glad to have something to do. I hardly saw Will at all today. We had dinner together, but he did homework at the table and then went straight upstairs to do more. He's got a big history test tomorrow. And…"

She hesitated, sitting down at the table. Alex sat down across from her and took a bite of casserole. "Truthfully," she went on, "I was glad for the distraction. I filled out the insurance paperwork today and it was kind of…depressing."

He stopped eating. "Holly, I'm sorry. That must have been awful."

"The paperwork part wasn't so bad. I even keep a household inventory in a safe deposit box, like the insurance companies tell you to but no one ever does. So the contents form was pretty easy to fill out...except..."

Her eyes filled with tears suddenly, which she did her best to blink back. "Sorry. But there was no place on the form for Will's baby pictures, or the drawings he brought home from kindergarten, or the Mother's Day card he made in third grade...or..."

He reached across the table and covered her hand with his.

"Sorry," she said again, taking a deep breath. "I know the important thing is that Will and I got out safely. It's just...everything's gone. The paper chains he made for the Christmas tree when he was seven—" She smiled through her tears. "Every year he begs me not to put them up, but it's not Christmas without them." Her smile faded. "The pictures are the worst, though. I have the more recent ones on my computer at work, but not Will's baby or toddler pictures. The ones I took before I had a digital camera. I always meant to have them scanned...but..."

"That's rough, Holly. I'm so sorry." He racked his brain, trying to think of some way to help. He hesitated. "Would your parents have any copies of those? Or... would Brian?"

She blinked in surprise. "To be honest, I hadn't even thought about that. Of course they might. It couldn't hurt to ask, right? My parents, anyway," she amended. "I don't enjoy talking with Brian at the best of times, and I really don't feel like dealing with him now. He doesn't even know about the fire yet, unless Will called him."

"Holly, why did you—" He stopped suddenly.

Holly waited a moment. "Why did I what?" she asked finally.

Alex shook his head. "It's not important." Without realizing it, he'd started to stroke the back of her hand with his thumb. Now he let her hand go as casually as he could. He knew from experience that even when he was touching her to offer comfort, his libido could get carried away.

"Okay, now I'm curious. What were you going to say?"

He shrugged. "It's just…talking about Brian made me wonder…"

"Wonder what?"

"The same thing I've wondered ever since high school," he admitted. "Why you ever went out with the guy. But you don't have to talk about it if you don't want to."

She shook her head at him, but she was smiling. "You always told me what a jerk he was."

"Yeah, and a lot of good that did. So what was the attraction?"

She sighed. "I only figured it out after things were over between us. After my parents kicked me out and I was on my own. Dating Brian was really more about them than me. I'd always worked so hard for their love, their acceptance, and Brian was exactly the kind of boyfriend they always wanted me to have. All form and no substance, just like them." She spoke a little bitterly, and Alex wished he'd kept his mouth shut.

"Hey, you don't—"

"No, it's okay. I don't mind you knowing what an idiot I was—especially since you knew already. You told me the truth about Brian from the beginning, and I never listened. All I did was hate you for it."

His heart contracted. "Holly, I—"

"It's okay," she said again, with a crooked smile. "I don't hate you anymore."

He couldn't find anything to say to that.

"By the way," she was saying now, "I found out something else when I was doing the forms. My insurance policy covers living expenses in the event of a loss. So Will and I could be out of here in a few days if…"

"You want to leave?" He was surprised at how much he hated the idea, even though he'd been thinking just a few hours ago about getting his sanity back once Holly and Will were gone.

She bit her lip. "It's not that I want to leave. You've been so great to Will and me…but we have to be cramping your style a little."

"What style? I don't have a style. You're not cramping anything. And why would you want to stay in a hotel or an apartment? You've got a whole house here."

"Your house," she reminded him. "And we are cramping your style, or at least your social life. You had a call from someone today. Just before you got home, actually."

Damn. "Who was it?"

"She said her name was Amber. I let the machine pick up, so you can listen to the message yourself." Her cheeks turned pink. "I had the impression she wanted to come see you. For an, um, overnight."

He leaned across the table for emphasis. "Listen to me, Holly. I'm not seeing anyone right now, and I don't plan to see anyone in the near future. Amber and I broke up more than a year ago. Maybe she was looking for a hookup, but I'm not. Okay? You and Will aren't cramping my style. And I'd like you to stay here." He pulled back a little. "If you want to, that is."

"I want to," she said. "I mean…if you're sure…."

Relief flooded through him. "I'm sure."

A smile spread across her face. "Okay, then, we'll stay. Until you get tired of us, that is."

Until he got tired of them? Holly and Will had been here two days, and already he could hardly imagine the house without them.

And Holly even looked beautiful under fluorescent kitchen lights.

She covered a yawn with her hand and rose to her feet. "It's getting late—I guess I should say good-night."

She went upstairs to her room and his mind flashed to the memory he'd tried to repress all day—the image of her lying in bed, drenched in moonlight, murmuring his name in her sleep.

He waited until he heard her bedroom door close before he went upstairs himself.

He could tell that the hallway and bathroom had been part of her cleaning spree, but when he opened the door to his bedroom, it was obvious she hadn't been in there. It felt a little depressing, stale and dusty and unloved.

The way his whole house would feel once she left.

It was a cool October evening, perfect football weather, and Holly sat in the stands next to Tom Washington's parents. She'd thought about Alex a fair amount last night and during work today, but for the last hour and a half she hadn't thought about him at all, even though he was right below her, clearly visible on the sidelines.

She was too busy thinking about the game.

The score was tied. There were three minutes to go in the fourth quarter, second down and eight with Weston on their own thirty-five yard line. For the twentieth time that night Holly jumped to her feet in outrage. "Did you *see* that?" she said to David and Angela Washington, waving her hand toward the field. "How could the ref miss that call? Pass interference! That should be a fifteen-yard penalty and an automatic first down."

"Not only that," Angela said, and if looks could kill there was one referee who would have been good and dead. "They roughed the passer, too. Charlie's still down."

It was true. A sudden hush fell over the crowd, home fans and visitors alike, as Weston's trainer trotted out onto the field to look at the Wildcats' starting quarterback, Charlie Mazillo, who was lying on his side clutching his left leg.

"Oh, no," David Washington said. "I think it's his knee."

Whatever it was, it had obviously ended the game for Charlie. He had to be helped off the field, leaning on his coach and his trainer, to a round of obligatory applause from the stands.

"Those *bullies*," Holly said furiously. "I can't believe they've been getting away with this kind of crap all night. My God, these are high school kids."

Angela shook her head. "Yes, but this is Ohio, and we play our football for blood."

"Alex doesn't," Holly said, her voice positive. "He plays to win, but he doesn't play dirty."

David sighed. "Alex is rare. He's a coach who plays the game the right way and can still maintain a winning record. Most of them can't manage that."

"And to think I was starting to *like* this game. Maybe I had the right idea all along."

"Hey," Angela said suddenly, looking down at the sidelines. "Coach is sending Will out there."

Holly gripped the other woman's hand in sudden panic. Her baby boy, going out on that field to face that gang of thugs?

Angela patted her on the back. "Don't worry. Will's tough, and he's smart. He can handle it."

"What do you mean he can handle it? He's fifteen years old. Charlie's a senior and *he* couldn't handle it."

"The referees will call a cleaner game after this. They'll have to."

"Oh, sure they will," Holly muttered, watching Will trot out to the huddle. Even from up here she could tell he was panicking, too. This wasn't a series or two in a game they already had sewn up. This was three minutes to go in a tie game, a game they'd only kept tied by the incredible play of their starting quarterback, who'd just been injured by a vicious hit from the Steeltown defense.

Will wasn't ready for this. Holly could read the uncertainty in his posture. It wasn't *fair,* she thought wildly. It was too much pressure to put on a fifteen-year-old boy.

Then he handed the ball off to Tom, who ran for twelve yards and a first down, and while David and Angela cheered for their son Holly breathed a sigh of relief. Maybe it would be okay. She no longer even cared about winning the game. She just wanted Will to get through this without getting hurt, and without making any huge mistakes that would torture him for the rest of—

She groaned and closed her eyes briefly. Will had just gotten sacked, and although he scrambled to his feet right away, obviously unhurt, she could tell he was rattled. The very next play he was called for intentional grounding, and in a flash of insight she knew he was afraid to pass the ball, afraid to touch the ball, afraid to have the game resting on his shoulders.

Alex called a time-out and Holly wondered what he would say. Will was probably hoping his coach would call another rushing play, and another and another, but then Tom would be the focus of the punishment the Steelers were handing out, and, anyway it wouldn't work. You had to balance your running attack with your passing attack if you wanted to have success—and that meant you needed a quarterback who believed in himself.

Alex was talking to Will by the sideline. Holly took a deep breath and let it out. She felt calmer suddenly, seeing them together. Alex would say the right things. Will trusted him. Will nodded at whatever his coach was saying, and Alex slapped him on the back. Then all the players came together for the team grip.

"Go Wildcats!" they said with one voice, and then they were running back out on the field.

The opposing teams lined up to face each other. The crowd noise made it impossible to hear but she could see Will behind center, looking right and left as he called the play, crisp confidence in his bearing as he took the snap and backpedaled in the pocket.

And the offensive line held as three wide receivers headed down the field. Will kept his head up, reading the defense, and freezing the safety in the middle of the field with a pump fake. Then he let the ball fly. And watched it sail downfield in a perfect spiral, right into the arms of the intended receiver, who gathered it in gleefully and scampered across the goal line for a touchdown.

They missed the extra point but nobody cared. By the time the Wildcats lined up to kick the ball off, there was still so much pandemonium in the stands that Holly couldn't hear her own voice as she shouted, pounding David and Angela on the back and arms and any place she could reach, and herself being pounded.

The wind had been knocked out of the Steelers and they couldn't do a thing with the ball. They turned it over on downs and then the Wildcats just held on grimly, running a series of safe, clock-killing plays until time ran out and the visiting crowd swept out on the field, carrying Holly with them, and she was so proud and happy and there was such joyful madness all around her that she didn't register that Alex had swept her up into his arms until he was spinning her around fast enough to make her dizzy.

"We did it!" he said, as if hardly able to believe it himself. He let her slide back to the ground but kept his arms around her, smiling down into her eyes, and she was so happy, and Alex was so happy, and her hands were still resting on his shoulders as she looked up at him. All of these things together made it seem perfectly natural to rise up on her toes and give him a quick kiss on the lips.

Later, when Holly was trying to analyze the incident rationally, she told herself that she had just meant it as a brief, friendly kiss, something celebratory stemming out of overflowing emotion and the general joy and craziness that was erupting all around them.

If so, that's not what it turned into.

Holly started to step back, but Alex's arms tightened almost convulsively around her waist, pulling her sharply against him. She gasped, and he let her go, but only so he could thrust his fingers into her hair and pull her to him for another kiss, parting her lips ruthlessly with his tongue and plundering her mouth, the taste of him sweeter and fiercer than anything she'd ever known.

In one instant Holly's entire world was reduced to this man, his hard body like steel against hers, her breasts crushed against his chest, his fingers tangled in her hair and his mouth bruising hers. She snaked her arms around his neck and pulled him even closer, opening herself to him completely, her tongue meeting his in a glorious, feverish tangle.

The sound of a trumpet blaring in her ear was like a bucket of cold water. Holly jumped and stumbled back a few steps with her hand to her heart.

It was the Weston High marching band, milling around chaotically as they prepared to lead a victory dance to the parking lot, and in the time it took to recover from the shock, Holly was reflecting that they'd probably saved her from seducing their coach in the middle of a football field surrounded by teenagers, their parents and several newspaper reporters.

Wouldn't that have made a nice front page photo for the *Weston Herald.*

Holly took a breath and looked around. In the general pandemonium it didn't look as if anyone had even noticed their little interlude, which couldn't have lasted more than ten seconds, and Will, thank goodness, was nowhere in sight.

She couldn't look at Alex. She put a hand up to her mouth, which she knew was swollen with the most incredible kiss she'd ever experienced, and wondered if she could possibly get away with just, you know, walking away as if nothing had—

"Holly," Alex said, grabbing her arm, and she risked a look at him. Whatever expression she'd expected to see on his face, it wasn't this. He looked worried. Not blasted with lust like her, or even just dazed by the suddenness of it all, but simply worried.

"Please don't be mad," he said, his voice sounding concerned, and all Holly could do was blink at him. "I didn't mean—it was just—" He floundered around for a while longer before Holly finally found her voice.

"The heat of the moment," she said, thinking that made as much sense as anything else. Whatever it had been, it obviously wasn't going to happen again, if Alex's current effort to backtrack was any indication, so the only thing to do was put this behind them with as little embarrassment and disruption to their friendship as possible.

"Right," he said, sounding relieved, and Holly felt a wave of depression. How could he be so relieved that they'd never be doing that again? Was she really that bad a kisser?

It wasn't her fault, she thought defensively. It wasn't as if she'd had a ton of practice. Not like he'd obviously had. God, the way that man could kiss… Holly's eyes fluttered closed at the memory and she had to bite her lip to keep from making a sound she was very much afraid would have been a moan.

"I've got to find Will," she said, clinging to something familiar.

"Will. Right. He was incredible tonight, Holly. A natural. It took real courage to do what he did tonight."

Courage. Something she knew nothing about, or she'd be throwing her arms around Alex instead of standing here like a half-wit. So what if she was a bad kisser. She could ask him to teach her, couldn't she?

Except that Alex didn't look like a man interested in teaching her anything. He looked more like a man embarrassed by a momentary indiscretion, precipitated by something she'd initiated, however innocently.

She had kissed him first, after all. Alex's response had probably been automatic for him, like his flirting. A woman kisses you and you respond. Like Pavlov's dogs.

She thought about all the girls he'd dated in high school, about the call from Amber, about what Rich Brennan had called "the Alex McKenna revolving door." She didn't want to be one of those women, with him for a few casual months and then gone. She wasn't wired that way. And Alex wasn't wired any other way.

"I've got to find Will," she said again, speaking carefully, like a drunk doing her best not to slur her words. She patted Alex on the arm, wanting to convey somehow that it was all right, that he didn't need to be embarrassed, that she understood. He looked unhappy, which was nice of him. In his own way he was a gentleman. He would have taken back the kiss if he could.

Which was the difference between them. Because even though she was embarrassed, too, even though what she was feeling now terrified her, Holly was glad it had happened. At least now she could say she'd had one great kiss in her lifetime. Every woman should be able to say that.

Even if it had only been great for her.

She had been there with him, Alex told himself over and over that night as he lay awake. The post-game celebration had seemed to go on for hours, but Alex had barely noticed it through the pain and confusion he was feeling now.

She'd been there with him. He was sure of it. The way she had leaned into his kiss… He'd never been turned on so hard and so fast in his life. She was so fiery, so passionate. If only she could let herself go….

But she couldn't. You'd think he'd know that by now. Holly had always shied away from expressing her passion, the passion Alex had always seen in her, the passion she was so careful to hide from the world.

It made sense, really. Holly was a person who needed to feel in control, and passion was about giving up control. She would never take kindly to a feeling that took her over, that swept her away, that put someone or something else in the driver's seat—even if it was only for a little while. Holly might be a smoldering flame but she would never, never let it show except in flashes. Once when she was drunk. Once when her house burned down. And once when her son had just won one of the most dramatic football games Alex had ever coached.

He'd come home to find the two of them there before him, Will still pumped up with adrenaline and excitement, telling his mom for what was probably the hundredth time how calm he had felt taking that snap, how he'd known, just *known,* he'd be able to complete the pass, how he hadn't let fear stop him. He'd seen Alex come in and jumped to his feet, the happiness bubbling out of him until Alex couldn't help but smile in response, in spite of the anxious look he shot at Holly.

"It really was an amazing game," she said, meeting his eyes with what looked like complete self-possesion. So much for his hope that she might still be affected by the mind-blowing kiss they'd shared. "So amazing that a person could possibly get carried away by all the emotion." She gave him a rueful look, her lips forming a silent "sorry" behind Will's back.

Alex gave her the universal forget-about-it gesture, a quick wave of the hand, and that was that.

The three of them spent the next two hours together talking and laughing, with Will doing most of each but Holly and Alex contributing more toward the end of the evening. The two adults were a little uncomfortable at first but slowly grew used to each other again until, finally, things felt almost back to normal.

Normal.

Alex sighed and scrubbed his face with his hands. Oh, he supposed it was better this way. It was what Holly wanted. Just because he wanted something different didn't mean it was going to happen. In fact, it was pretty clear now it was never going to happen. A woman who could walk away from a kiss like that was not a woman he'd be able to talk into anything, especially if it went against her better judgment.

And her judgment was probably right. He was more attracted to her than he'd ever been to any woman, but that wouldn't be—shouldn't be—enough for Holly. She was a woman who deserved forever, and he didn't do forever. The most he'd ever offered a woman was a few months of fun.

Holly deserved more than that. She deserved everything a man had to offer, including his heart. And that was something Alex had never offered to anyone.

So it was all for the best, right? They were both cowards when it came to love.

Not that this was about love, of course.

There was heat between them, even if Holly refused to face it, but there wasn't love. Friendship, yes. Respect and affection, yes. A deep connection, yes—for him, anyway. And a long-standing crush that he had, apparently, never gotten over.

But love was about forever. And when it came to Holly, it was about Will, too. What in his track record would give anyone, including him, the idea that he was ready for love and commitment with a single mother and her teenage son?

No. Holly had been right to run from their kiss, even if she'd run out of fear. Alex had never believed in listening to fear, but when it came to his feelings for Holly, he was prepared to make an exception.

Saturday morning was Pancake Day, Will and Holly informed him when he came downstairs at ten o'clock. By the looks of things they'd already done some damage pancake-wise, and Holly was at the stove flipping three more. She grinned at him, wearing jeans and his Bengals jersey. Her hair was in a loose braid down her back.

"What did you do, raid my T-shirt drawer?"

She looked down. "Oh, right. Sorry. This is one of the shirts you brought me that first night. They're so comfortable, and when I went shopping last week I sort of concentrated on work clothes and didn't really get anything casual. Is it all right if I borrow it a little longer? This one and the Pittsburgh one? Just until I can get a few of my own."

He waved it away. He was getting pretty good at that. *Don't worry, it's as if it never happened, what's a little toe-curling kiss among friends?*

"No problem," he said out loud. "Comfort is important." He cleared his throat. "So what are you two doing today? Anything exciting planned?"

"I'm going to teach my mom to throw a football."

Alex gave Holly a skeptical look as he dug into the huge pile of pancakes she put in front of him, which were, predictably, delicious. "Are you telling me you actually *want* to learn to throw a football?"

Holly grinned. "I wouldn't say I'm brimming over with excitement, but in case you hadn't noticed it's a gorgeous fall day out there and running around in your enormous backyard has its appeal. I'm going to the gym later, too. I haven't been since the fire, which is a mistake. Missing workouts always makes me cranky. My job is good for intellectual stimulation but not physical stimulation. I need both."

Alex tried not to think of the physical stimulation he'd like to give Holly. He was turning into one of those guys who had a sexual thought every seven seconds and couldn't say two words without one of them sounding like an innuendo.

He sighed. "I have about an acre of leaves to rake. I'll keep you company."

Will looked delighted. "That's great! We'll help you rake after we throw some passes. That's good exercise, too, right, Mom?"

"Fine with me. I like creating order out of chaos, as you know. Raking is a very satisfying job. You start with a yard full of messy leaves and end up with tidy piles. Just my kind of thing."

Holly was right: it was a gorgeous day. Blue, blue sky, and maple trees all around with leaves like flames. The colors looked as if they'd been drawn by a child: bright gold, brilliant red, burnt orange. The neighbors next door were burning leaves and the sharp, acrid scent drifted on the wind, mixing with the cold clean smell of the air and the dry sweet smell of the leaves everywhere, on the trees, underfoot, fluttering down onto their shoulders.

Holly was looking autumnal herself, with her copper-colored hair and the brown sweater she'd put on.

The raking was forgotten as the three of them ran around like little kids, occasionally tossing the football back and forth but mostly just running, spinning, taking in huge cleansing breaths of the autumn air.

After a half an hour of that Will decided it was time to get serious. "Okay, Mom, Alex will show you how to throw a spiral pass and I'll be your receiver. Your hands are kind of small but I know you can do it." He took off at a trot, stopping at a distance Holly thought was well beyond the point she might hope to heave a football.

The sunlight was brilliant and Holly squinted across the yard at her son. "He's delusional," she said as Alex handed her the football.

"He just has faith in you. You should be flattered. Now grip the ball with your fingers on the laces and plant that back foot like we talked about. Cock your arm back and—no, not like that."

"What do you mean, not like that? What am I doing wrong?"

He should just show her, like he would one of his players. Of course that would involve touching her, which would be bad. Or good. Or—oh, what the hell. He came up behind her and adjusted her arm position. "Like that, see? Much better. Now turn your upper body. Keep your eyes downfield. Good!"

Alex let himself enjoy the contact for just a moment

before he took a step back. "Okay, now, let it fly. Concentrate on your mechanics." He watched critically as she made her first attempt. "All right, kid! Not bad!" He reached up for a high five and she slapped his hand in triumph as her pass made it close to where Will was, so that by running forward he could catch it easily.

"Hey, this is fun!" she said incredulously, smiling radiantly at Alex.

"You're adorable," he said before he could stop himself, and she blushed, but he hadn't messed anything up because she was still grinning over her success when Will trotted back to them. The next few hours passed in a happy blur of running, passing and kicking, until the three of them threw themselves down under a maple tree to rest, staring up at the patterns of branches and flaming leaves against the azure sky.

"I feel so happy right now," Will said after several minutes of companionable silence. "It almost hurts in my chest, I'm so happy. Has that ever happened to you?"

Holly laughed. "Once or twice in my long life. How about you, Alex?"

"Once or twice." He fell silent, looking up at the leaves fluttering in the breeze, the restful quiet all around punctuated by bird calls, sharp and sweet. "I'm on Will's side about today," he said after a few minutes. "This is pretty perfect."

"Can we stay here forever?" Will asked.

Yes, Alex wanted to say.

"Well, not forever," Holly said, and when Alex turned his head he saw her scrambling to her feet, brushing leaves off her jeans. She wasn't looking at him. "In fact, I should get to the gym if I want to work out today."

She smiled goodbye and walked back toward the house, leaving Will and Alex in the exact same positions they'd been in, under the exact same tree and the exact same sky, except that some of the golden sparkle seemed to have gone out of the afternoon.

Chapter Eight

On Tuesday, Will came to a decision.

He couldn't figure out why his mom and Alex were taking so long to get together, until it occurred to him that *he* might be a factor. After all, they were all living here, and his mom could be kind of old-fashioned. Chances were, she wouldn't feel comfortable letting anything happen with Alex while he was around.

Well, okay. He could fix that.

Tom mentioned that he and his dad were going on a fishing trip over the weekend, and Will asked if he could go along.

He decided to announce his plans Friday morning, so his mom wouldn't have any time to adjust or come up with a counter plan. Not only was she old-fashioned, but when it came to anything emotional—her own emotions, anyway—she wasn't exactly brave. He didn't want her to find a way to duck out of a weekend alone with Alex.

In the meantime, the days were falling into a familiar pattern: school, football and dinners at home.

The dinners were fun. So fun, in fact, that Will started to wonder if maybe his mom and his coach had the right idea. Maybe friendship was the way to go, after all.

Then he caught Alex looking at his mom one night when the three of them were watching a football film.

"I like this," Holly said suddenly, causing Alex to jump guiltily.

"What?" he asked, trying to sound as if he hadn't been staring at her for the last ten minutes.

"Football," she said, her eyes on the screen. "It's like financial planning. Lots of strategy and taking the long view, but also reacting to what's happening in the present moment. Making a game plan and sticking to the broader goals you want to achieve, but being willing to explore different ways to achieve them if what you're doing isn't working."

Alex looked surprised. "That's exactly how I look at football. At least the game-planning part." He paused for a moment. "I can't believe I'm about to say this, but you've been such a good sport about all this football stuff I feel like it's only fair to show a little interest in what you do. Tell me about financial planning. If anyone could make it sound interesting, you could."

Holly turned to look at him, and there was a glint in her eye that Will recognized.

"What?" Alex asked warily.

"That pit of chaos you call an office. You'll notice I haven't so much as crossed the threshold on one of my 'cleaning sprees' as you call them. I've stuck to the common areas and respected your right to live like a college student in your bedroom and your office."

"And I appreciate it," he said even more warily.

"Well, no more," she said. "At least, I guess you can still have your bedroom, but we're going to organize that office until it resembles a human habitat and then, my friend, we're going to balance your checkbook, examine the state of your finances, discuss your long-term goals and risk tolerance, and come up with a personalized financial strategy for you. No, don't thank me. It's the least I can do after you gave me and Will a place to stay. Really, it's my pleasure."

She was grinning, and Will knew his coach was sunk. Apparently he knew it, too.

"How long will it take?" Alex asked, resigned.

"Hours and hours," she said cheerfully. "Days probably. There's no game this week, right? So you're not as busy as usual. We'll get started tonight."

As Alex reluctantly followed a determined Holly out of the room, Will shook his head. Financial planning. How many more ways could they come up with to avoid dealing with what was right in front of them? He was starting to wonder if even leaving them alone together this weekend would do the trick. Oh, well, all he could do was hope for the best.

Why did adults always make everything so complicated?

On Friday morning, Holly got up early to make breakfast. She'd been doing that all week, telling herself it was because she wanted to be the one sending her son off to school with a nice hot meal inside him instead of the other way around. In truth, it was also because she liked seeing Alex before they went to work. After all, eventually she and Will would be moving out, however settled they seemed to be here. Her meetings yesterday with an architect and a firm of contractors was a reminder that their stay here was temporary. Holly intended to soak up as much Alex as she could before then.

Five minutes after her son came downstairs, that suddenly seemed like a bad idea.

"I'm going away this weekend," Will said casually, as if it was nothing, as if he wasn't about to remove her best defense against the feelings she still entertained for Alex, late at night in the privacy of her bedroom. The feelings she couldn't possibly act on because of the fifteen-year-old down the hall.

"What do you mean you're going away?" she demanded. "You can't tell me this on Friday morning." She glared at Alex. "Do you know anything about this?" He shook his head, clearly as taken aback as she was, and she turned back to her son. "Kindly explain to me exactly where you think you're going."

Will took a bite of oatmeal. "Tom and his dad asked me yesterday. I forgot to mention it till now. You can call Mr. Washington if you want, to clear it. We're going camping. We're leaving right after school."

"Tonight? You're going to be gone tonight?" Holly felt panic rising and briefly considered asking if she could go along.

"Tonight and tomorrow night. We'll be back Sunday afternoon." He picked up a cinnamon roll, his expression cheerful.

Holly cleared her throat. "You know, I haven't been camping since I was a little girl. Do you think Tom's dad would—"

"Nope. Sorry. It's kind of a guy thing. Also the tent's only big enough for three. Besides, you guys have all that financial planning to do. And it's supposed to rain. You'd be miserable out there."

"Why won't *you* be miserable?" Holly asked, knowing she was beaten but still clinging to a straw.

Will grinned. "We're planning to do a lot of fishing. Fish bite great when it's raining. I'm all packed and everything, Mom. I can bring my duffel bag on the bus so you don't need to worry about a thing." He got to his feet and gave a jaunty wave. "Have a great weekend, you two. See you Sunday."

And before she could think of anything else to say, he was gone.

The silence felt a little awkward. Holly was sitting at the kitchen table, frowning down at her cinnamon roll, and wondering what Alex was thinking. Probably he didn't care much. Why should he? They were friends.

"Will's right," she said brightly, forcing herself to meet Alex's eyes with a cheerful smile. "A rainy weekend will be the perfect chance to concentrate on your finances."

The smile wavered a little at Alex's expression. He was leaning back in his chair, his head cocked to one side, his blue eyes speculative.

"Okay, it's time for me to get going," she added, her mind working quickly. Dinner tonight might not be a great idea. "I'm meeting some friends after work, so go ahead and have dinner without me. I'll be home late. I probably won't see you till tomorrow morning. We can start talking about your investment portfolio then."

Alex frowned. "I don't have an investment portfolio."

"Not yet, you don't. That's all about to change."

Alex shook his head at her and she grinned at him, delighted that things seemed to be back to normal. See? She didn't need Will around to keep her from making a pass at Alex. She could rely on her maturity and good judgment.

She held on to that thought all day at work, and later during dinner at her desk with a paperback for company, and still later as she drove home. By the time she pulled into Alex's driveway, she was actually starting to believe it.

Holly turned off her engine and sat in the warmth of her car for a few minutes, listening to the rain drum against the windows. It sure was coming down. She hoped that Will and Tom and David were warm and dry in their tent.

Of course she'd left too quickly this morning to stop and think about grabbing a raincoat or umbrella. It had been all right earlier, when it was just starting to drizzle, but now it was pouring, Alex's driveway wasn't all that close to his front door, and she was going to get drenched.

She sighed. At least if she came into the house wet and cold, she'd have an excuse to go straight up to her room if Alex happened to be downstairs.

Holly took a breath, ducked her head and opened the door. A blast of rain hit her and she ran for the house. She'd almost made it when something tripped her up and she went down, sprawling, in the flower bed beside the front walkway.

"Great," she muttered, preparing to get muddily to her feet, when a soft, sad bark halted her movement.

Her own woebegone state forgotten, Holly peered around to see where the sound had come from.

A pair of big, sad dog eyes looked at her from underneath the porch.

"Come on out of there, sweetheart," she coaxed, kneeling down despite the pelting rain and the further damage to her beige wool pantsuit.

Another soft bark. It was a young dog, maybe a puppy.

"Come on out, baby. We've got raccoons under there who'd eat a little pup like you for breakfast. Come out and we'll—"

"Who are you talking to? And why are you crawling around in the mud?"

It was Alex, standing on the front porch.

"I heard a dog barking," she said defensively, raising her voice to be heard over the wind and the rain. "He's under the porch. I'm just trying to get him out so we can take him inside."

"And we want to take him inside because…?"

"He'll be the first animal we take on board when we build our ark," she said, glaring at him. "Why do you think? It's storming out here, in case you hadn't noticed. No one should be out on a night like this, especially not a puppy. He's lost and he sounds scared. Show some compassion."

Alex sighed in resignation. "Food will probably lure him out. I'll go get something."

While Alex was gone Holly spoke softly to the dog, getting him used to the sound of her voice. Then Alex was there, crouching down beside her in the rain, holding out some leftover chicken and talking almost as gently as she was.

"It's okay, buddy. You lucked out. This woman is a sucker for a sob story. We'll fill your tummy with leftovers if you come on inside with us."

Slowly, the owner of the eyes emerged, revealing what appeared to be a Labrador puppy, all black, shivering with the cold and wet and eyeing Alex hopefully.

"Food inside," he said, standing up and backing away toward the house. When the puppy came forward, tail wagging, Holly gathered him into her arms and followed Alex up the stairs.

"There," she said triumphantly as Alex closed the door behind them. "See how easy that was?"

"Sure," he said as he dripped on the hall floor. He shook his head, but he was smiling at her and the dog she held tightly against her chest. "I'll go get some towels. Try to keep our new friend in this general area, will you? And check to see if he's wearing a collar."

He was.

"It says Johnny Peterson, 43 Linden Rd," Holly told him a few minutes later as they were toweling off the puppy and themselves. Johnny seemed to appreciate the attention, as well as the big bowl of chicken scraps Alex put down in front of him. "That's the lady next door, right? The nice one who lent me the jeans."

"Yep. Her name's Anna. I'll give her a call." He looked at her. "Why are you always in my house looking like a disaster victim? Maybe you should go change into something a little less muddy."

Holly made a face at him but followed his suggestion, running upstairs to put on jeans and a sweatshirt and a pair of sneakers. When she came back down Alex was wrestling with Johnny in the hall.

"She's home, she's frantic, she's been looking everywhere, she can't thank us enough. I'm going to drive over there right now."

"I'd like to come, too."

"But you're actually clean and dry now. Why don't you stay here? I'll be back in a few minutes."

Holly shook her head. "I like Johnny. And who's going to snuggle him while you drive? I'm coming."

"He could probably last two minutes in the car without dying of snuggle deprivation," Alex said, but he handed her a raincoat and the two of them headed out the door, with Johnny a warm, happy, wriggling bundle in Holly's arms.

Anna really couldn't thank them enough. She was in her fifties, the last of an old Scandinavian farming family, and Holly was so charmed by her she might have stayed an hour if Alex hadn't stood up to go. "We should probably head back so we can change into dry clothes," he said, and Anna instantly agreed.

"Of course, of course. You'll have to come for dinner some night this week. Homemade chicken pot pie."

"Sounds wonderful," Holly said. She got down on one knee to say goodbye to Johnny, who covered her face in enthusiastic dog kisses until she was laughing so hard she fell over backward.

"Holly may ask for visitation rights," he told Anna. "I think she's attached to your dog."

"Well, Johnny seems attached to her," Anna said, smiling up at him. "She seems like an easy person to get attached to."

Alex reached out a hand to help Holly to her feet. "She has her moments," he admitted.

The rain was coming down in sheets as the two of them ran from Anna's front door to Alex's car. The wind was starting to pick up, too. In the five seconds it took to make it into the front seat, they were soaked.

It was even worse when they pulled into Alex's

driveway. As soon as Holly stepped out of the car the wind snatched her hood and blew it back off her head, exposing her to the full fury of the storm.

Holly laughed out loud, suddenly exhilarated. She held out her arms and spun around, almost dancing, her face turned up to the sky and her eyes squeezed shut. She was one with the storm, with the rain, with the wind. It was glorious.

Alex made it to the porch and turned to see what had become of Holly. She was standing out there in the storm, looking up into the wild black sky with her arms outstretched, laughing as the rain lashed against her. With her long red hair streaming out behind her and every inch of her soaked, she looked like a water witch out of some seafaring folktale.

"Hey there, crazy lady, get the heck inside!" Alex shouted over the rising wind and thundering rain. She flashed a grin at him and ran for the door he was holding open. The two of them practically fell into the front hallway, panting and dripping and shivering, and Alex slammed the door shut behind them.

He flicked on the light switch, and the old-fashioned chandelier shed its dim, crystalline light over Holly, her face glowing from the wet and the cold. She stood there breathing hard and deeply, her green eyes enormous and filled with laughter. She let her dripping raincoat slide to the floor and shook her head like a dog shedding water, giggling when Alex got a spray of droplets in his face.

She was so beautiful. In his whole life he'd never seen anything to equal her. She was like that woman in the story, the one with the seven veils. Just when you thought you'd seen every side of her, you realized you hadn't even begun.

She was twisting her hair now to wring out the rain-water, and she looked like a mermaid. Alex was the sailor watching her, knowing he could never have her, knowing she lived in a world he would never be allowed to enter.

Except she wasn't some unattainable nymph out of a fairy tale. She was flesh and blood, and he wanted her. Everything in him was distilled into that wanting, the desire to make love to her until she forgot everything but the fire that burned between them.

He took two quick strides until he was close enough to touch her, and Holly looked up in surprise.

Alex was beside her so suddenly Holly was startled, and then the expression on his face froze her where she stood. Her heart began to pound. When he began to walk forward, slowly and deliberately, she found herself backing up until she was pressed up against the inside of the front door.

The electricity between them seemed to crackle in the air, an echo of the storm outside.

"How do you do that?" he asked her, his voice low.

"Do what? What are you talking about?" Holly's eyes were wide as she stared at him, knowing now, when it was too late, that she'd been a fool to think she could bury her attraction to this man.

"This," he said, looking at her, at the water that clung to her hair, her lips, her lashes. "You play it safe and I go along with it, because I think that's what you want, and then you dance out in that storm like…" He paused, searching for the words he wanted. "There's something elemental about you, Holly. It's hidden most of the time, but it's there. You let it out once in a while, and then you cover it right back up. Something primal. Untamed."

Holly didn't like the sound of that. "I like to think of myself as very tame," she objected, trying for a light tone. "Polished and refined."

Alex shook his head. "I know you do. That's what's so funny. You wear these conservative outfits and you think you're fooling everyone. Even yourself. Hell, it probably works most of the time. But I've never been fooled. Even back in high school I wasn't fooled, and I still let you lie to me and to yourself, over and over again, and never did a damn thing about it."

It was getting harder to breathe. Desire was making her tremble, and if she didn't get away right now, Alex would know.

"I think I'll go and—" she started to say, taking a step sideways, but in a flash Alex's arms had trapped her, his hands flat against the door.

"Not until we finish this conversation," he said.

"What conversation? This isn't a conversation. This is—"

"This is me finally telling you the truth and you finally listening."

His blue eyes had never been more intense as they bored into hers, unyielding in their challenge. The planes of his face looked harsh and dangerous and his rain-soaked hair made him seem… What was the word he'd used before?

Elemental.

"Stop it," she whispered.

"Make me," he said roughly. "You know you can if you want to. Push me away. Better yet, just tell me you're not attracted to me. If you can do that, I'll walk away." He pulled back a little. "Can you do that?"

She could. She had to. Because if she gave in to these feelings, her life would never be the same again.

She opened her mouth to say the words, but nothing came out.

He pushed away from the door, backing off a few paces, but his eyes never left hers.

"You can't do it. But you can't reach out for what you want, either." He took a step back toward her. "You're scared. And you're letting fear make your decisions for you."

Another step. "I've been scared, too. I've been scared since the night we kissed. But I'm damned if I'm going to let either of us run away again. Not without a fight, anyway. So go ahead, Holly. Give me all you've got. All the reasons why we can't do this."

One more step, and he was so close she couldn't think, couldn't breathe, couldn't see anything but him. He leaned in until his mouth was at her ear, and when he spoke his breath sent shivers down her spine.

"Come on, Holly. I'm sure you can think of just one reason."

At last she found her voice. "Stop it, Alex! I can't think when you're…when you're like this. You're too close. It's not a fair fight!" Even as she said the words she heard their absurdity, but Alex just smiled grimly.

"A fair fight is exactly what it is. What we've always had. We've been fighting each other from the moment we met, and you'd think we'd have figured out by now that neither one of us is going to win. Why the hell can't you see that? What are you so afraid of?"

There was something in his eyes Holly recognized.

He was daring her, damn him, just like he'd done back in high school.

He shook his head. "I guess you really are too much of a coward to go after what you want."

He paused, and when he spoke again, his voice was different, calmer and somehow more dangerous. "Unless it's in your dreams, right, Holly? Because you do dream me. I heard you last week, through your door. I went in and you were asleep, calling out my name again and again. And from the tone of your voice, I'd say whatever was happening in that dream, you were enjoying it."

Holly was so furious and so embarrassed that she finally found the strength to push past him, turning so he was between her and the door and she could face him with a little breathing room.

"How could you do something like that?" she spat out, her cheeks burning. "Come into my bedroom, listen to me talking in my sleep. How could you invade my privacy like that?"

Alex didn't give any ground. "Why not?" he asked. "You've invaded mine. You've invaded every part of me. Every nerve, every cell in my body. You think I don't dream about *you?*"

He walked toward her again, but this time Holly didn't back up. She knew this was her last stand. She held her head high, jaw clenched and nostrils flaring, and her eyes flashed as they met his.

"I want you, Holly," he said, and for the first time she saw the yearning behind his passion. "I want you like I've never wanted anything in my life. And you want me. But the only time you let us be together is when you're alone in your bed at night. Do you think about me then? What it would be like if I put my hands on you the way I want to?"

And suddenly Holly realized something.

He hadn't put his hands on her. Not tonight. He was battering at her defenses, but he hadn't used the one weapon she couldn't have resisted. If he'd grabbed her and kissed her like he had after Will's game, she would have surrendered without a fight. She would have been his for the taking.

But he didn't want that. He didn't want to take.

Holly closed her eyes. She felt something surging through her, an electricity so bright and fierce it made everything else fall away.

Alex was still talking, but she didn't care. She'd thought of one sure way to shut him up.

Alex never finished his last sentence. Holly put her hands on his chest and pushed, and he was so surprised he lost his balance, stumbling backward until he crashed up against the front door. Before he could recover she was there, against him, and then her mouth was pressed to his, fierce and desperate and clumsy.

For a second Alex was stunned into immobility. Then he was kissing her back, and he was so crazy for her and so terrified she would change her mind that he lifted her up and spun them so their positions were reversed, trapping her between the door and his body, shuddering when she wrapped her legs around his waist, and never for one second taking his mouth away from hers.

She tasted like rain, like heat, like Holly. His hunger was making him savage, his mouth crushing hers, but she was kissing him back just as fiercely. If the door hadn't been there to hold them up Alex would have fallen to his knees.

She was so raw, so passionate, this woman he'd dreamed about for so long and never, never thought he'd have. Now he was tasting her, feeling her, the heat between them so intense it seemed to burn through the layers of wet denim that separated them.

He broke the kiss and pressed his lips to her throat, right at her pulse point. She gasped and let her head fall back, her fingers digging into his shoulders hard enough to bruise.

He had to be inside her. Now. But they couldn't go upstairs to one of the beds. Alex was afraid to take the time, afraid she'd slip away from him somehow, change her mind, push him away. He'd wanted her for so long and now she was his, for as long as he could hold her— and he wasn't going to let her go.

He lowered them to the floor right where they were, pulling away only long enough to tug off his still-damp sweatshirt.

Then he turned back to her. His heart was pounding so hard the rush of blood in his ears drowned out the storm outside. With shaking hands he pulled her wet top over her torso and arms until she was free, and the only thing in his way was her cotton bra.

They reached for the front clasp at the same time. Their hands bumped, and their mutual clumsiness made them laugh in surprise. "Let me," Alex whispered, his eyes on hers, and somehow he managed to unhook the tiny piece of metal so the thin barrier fell away, and then his hands were cupped around her perfect breasts, her nipples pebbled against his palms.

Holly gasped, arching her back, and Alex lowered his

head. He grazed his teeth across one nipple and flicked the other back and forth with his thumb until Holly writhed against him, her hands fisting in his hair as she moaned his name.

That sound broke the last of his restraint.

But before he could move to take off her wet jeans Holly had unzipped them herself and was working them down her legs, her teeth sunk in her lower lip as she concentrated. Alex had to tear his eyes away in order to focus on his own clothes, losing pants and shoes and boxers in one damp heap. Then he remembered his wallet. He reached for his jeans again to grab it out of the back pocket, and thanked every deity he could when he found the condom inside.

In a second he was sheathed and could turn back to Holly.

He could hardly believe how beautiful she was. She was naked, stretched out on his hallway floor gazing up at him with her lips parted, her red hair curling damply around her bare shoulders and a flush of heat staining her cheeks. She reached for him, getting her hands on his shoulders and tugging him down to her, and when he hesitated just a moment, fighting for control so he wouldn't come before he even touched her, she arched up into him.

"Please, Alex," she said raggedly, her green eyes enormous. "Don't tease me. I need you...need you inside me."

Her words were fuel to a fire. Alex liked foreplay, the kind that went on for hours, but right now he'd be lucky if he lasted two minutes. And besides, he told himself as he positioned himself at her entrance, he and Holly had already had about eighteen years of foreplay. He wasn't going to wait one more second.

He thrust inside her, hard and deep, and the shock reverberated through both their bodies.

He went still. No woman had ever felt like this. He stared down at her, every muscle in his body taut, and saw she was frozen like he was, her eyes wide with the astonished awe he knew was mirrored in his own.

Then she was moving against him, her fingernails raking down his chest as she moaned. Her hips arched up against his and he couldn't stop himself from rocking into her again.

Alex's jaw clenched as he tried to go slow, knowing he didn't have long. But Holly was gripping his arms, her legs wrapped around him, and she was gasping, "Not slow—Alex, please—" And then he was driving into her with all the passion of repressed desire, his rhythm hard and fierce and brutally possessive, and Holly was biting her lips to keep from screaming.

Her eyes flew open and she stared at him, panting, and he saw the very moment she fell over the edge, her body jerking beneath him and her head arching back, and then she did scream, calling out his name, and the sound pulled him over the cliff with her as he came, harder than he thought possible, collapsing on top of Holly as he fought for breath and the world shattered around him.

It took a long, long time to come back to earth. As soon as he could move again Alex rolled over onto his side so he wouldn't crush the woman lying spent and lovely beneath him, drawing her close and wrapping her up tight, as if he intended to hold on to her forever.

It was an endless time before Holly could move again. It might have been hours. It seemed to take at least that long for her heart rate to slow and her breathing to return to some semblance of normal. Cradled against Alex's chest she could hear his heartbeat better than her own, as it slowed gradually to a strong, regular rhythm.

She kept her eyes shut, not wanting this moment to end, until the contrast between the warmth of Alex's body and the cold floor beneath her became uncomfortable and she began to long for a bed, a warm, soft bed they could burrow into and hibernate in till spring.

But to say that out loud seemed presumptuous.

As Holly felt the wonderful sexual haze start to dissipate, she pressed herself closer to Alex in an effort to recapture the warmth. He responded immediately, his arms tightening around her and one hand moving to stroke her hair.

It should have been reassuring.

Holly hid her face against Alex's broad chest, which was ironic considering he was a big part of her fears, the fears that were flooding back now as if they'd just been waiting in the wings, driven out of her mind by earth-shaking sex. Probably they'd go away permanently if she could make love with Alex forever, but physically it just wasn't possible. She could barely move her arms and legs now.

She took a deep breath to steady herself, but then she was inhaling the clean male scent of Alex, soap and rain and the faint tang of salty sweat, and she had to close her eyes.

What did *he* think about what had just happened? He had talked about wanting her, about lust and desire, but he hadn't said anything about…

Holly stopped herself in time. Don't even *think* that

word, she admonished herself. The only thing that had happened here was great sex. The only thing Alex had promised her was great sex.

And boy, had he delivered. Only a fool would go scrambling for more right now. Alex wasn't the ever-after kind of guy. He was danger and volatility and mind-blowing lust, and while those things might be amazing, they didn't usually come attached to a Hallmark card and a bottle of Chianti.

Alex was a great friend—unless they'd just messed that up tonight—and an unbelievable lover, but it would be asking way too much to expect him to be a boyfriend, too. It would go against his nature.

Holly turned her head so her cheek was pressed against Alex's chest and she could hear his heartbeat again. She didn't really want a boyfriend right now, anyway. Especially not one like Alex, who could fog her brain just by looking in her direction. She needed her mind clear right now. She had a job to focus on, and a son to take care of, and a destroyed home to recreate for both of them.

If she let herself rely on Alex for things he couldn't provide, it wouldn't be fair to either of them. Who knew better than she did that the moment you let yourself get comfortable was usually the moment you got the rug jerked out from under you? And honestly, she didn't think she could take it if that happened again. She had to make herself remember who and what Alex was. He was a good friend to her and to her son, but when it came to man-woman stuff he was nitroglycerin, the kind you left in the bottle if you valued your peace of mind.

A sudden visceral memory of Alex thrusting into

her made her wonder, briefly, if peace of mind might be overrated, but then she thought about Brian—how much she'd trusted him, and how he'd cracked when she'd given him more than he could handle. And Mark, too—in the end, he hadn't wanted to deal with the burdens that went with dating a single mother.

If she tried to force Alex into a role he couldn't possibly fill, they'd both suffer for it. And she didn't want to suffer like that again.

The cold floorboards, and the cold air against her bare skin, was starting to seep into her bones. Time to end this.

She used Alex for leverage to push herself to a sitting position.

"Hey!" he said immediately, sitting up with her and capturing her hands in his. "Where do you think you're going?"

She hesitated and saw him tense again. Well, he might not like it, but the sooner she made it clear where things stood, the better.

"I'm going to bed," she said quietly. "Alone. I think it would be better that way."

Alex rose to his feet and reached down a hand to help her up. Once she was standing he kept hold of her hand, stroking her wrist with his thumb.

"I knew it," he said, sounding almost resigned.

"Knew what?" she asked as she tried to pull her hand gently away from his.

"Knew you'd run away." He stood looking at her, and Holly felt a wave of guilt.

"Listen," he said, drawing her closer. "Let's save this part until the morning. It's traditional. If in the harsh light of day you feel the need to turn your back on what we obviously have going here, fine. But, please, Holly—at least give me tonight. Just one night. Please."

There was no way she could say no to him. Holly was momentarily terrified that she'd never be able to say no to him ever again, but she put that thought aside for now. One night really wasn't too much to ask.

"No sex," she warned him.

"No sex," he repeated. "That's fine. I may never be able to have sex again, anyway. I think you broke me."

Holly grinned, suddenly liking him so much it warmed her all over. "Oh, I think you'll live to love again. Think of all the disappointment among the female population of Ohio if you retired this young."

He looked at her a little quizzically, but he bit back whatever he had been going to say. "Let's sleep in your bed tonight," he said instead as they climbed the stairs together.

"Sure," Holly said, surprised. "How come?"

"It's warmer," he said as they walked down the hall and into her room.

"Warmer? Why?"

"Because it's yours," he said simply. Holly looked at him for a moment, not sure how to respond. Then she disappeared quickly into the bathroom.

Alex sighed. *Don't think about it,* he told himself as he lay down on Holly's bed, turning his head to breathe in the scent of her shampoo that lingered on her pillow. Don't think about tomorrow. Hell, tomorrow a meteor might strike the earth, destroying all life on this planet and his minor relationship problems along with it.

Just think about tonight.

He heard her footsteps and switched on the bedside

lamp, turning to see the soft light glowing against her bare skin. "You're so beautiful," he couldn't help saying as she came toward him, and even across the room he could tell she was blushing. He lifted the covers so she could slip under them, and when he felt how cold she was he wrapped her up in the fluffy quilts, tucking her in close to him so his own body heat could seep into her, as well.

Not to mention the fact that feeling Holly's soft skin and sexy curves pressed against him was extremely pleasant.

"Mmm," she said as she snuggled into him, and that was pleasant too. Alex let his eyes drift closed, just enjoying the moment.

"Where'd you get the condom?" Holly asked suddenly, and the question was so unexpected that Alex laughed. "I'm serious," she said, although he could tell she was smiling. "I mean, one second you're naked, and the next second you've got a condom on, like Superman coming out of a phone booth. Well, maybe not quite like that," she amended as he laughed again.

"I had it in my wallet."

"You keep a condom in your wallet?"

"Fortune favors the prepared," he said gravely, and she swatted at him.

"I suppose I shouldn't be surprised. I was thinking the other day you probably get lucky every week. Maybe every night." Her tone made it a question, but Alex deliberately didn't answer it. He just let his smile grow broader.

Finally she sighed in exasperation. "Look, just tell me. Give me a number. How many women have you been with during the last three months?"

He made a show of thinking about it, counting softly

under his breath, until she swatted him again. "Okay, okay," he said, grinning. "One."

She stared at him. "You've only slept with one woman besides me during the last three months?"

He held her gaze. "No, Holly. Only you."

"Oh," she said, blinking in surprise.

They were lying on their sides, facing each other, and Alex ran a finger down her forehead to the tip of her nose. "New topic," he said. "Let's talk about our greatest sexual experiences ever. I'll tell you mine and you can tell me yours. You first."

She pillowed her hand under her cheek. "I'm not about to make your head any bigger," she said severely.

"I just want to hear you say it," he persisted, grinning.

She sighed with exaggerated patience. "Fine," she said. "If you insist on having your ego stroked. On a scale of one to ten you were a hundred and three. Anything else you need me to tell you?"

He hid his grin this time. "That's good for now," he said, and then deliberately didn't say anything else until she poked him in the chest.

"Don't you dare," she warned him. "I have limited sexual experience and my self-esteem is precarious. You will immediately begin complimenting me in extravagant terms or there will be consequences."

He let his grin show then, but almost immediately it began to fade as he traced the side of her face with the palm of his hand.

"I don't think there are words," he said, and his voice was serious. "I've dreamed about what it would be like with you, and even my wildest fantasies fell short. I've never experienced anything even close to that with anyone else. You…" He paused and then smiled again. "I thought you were a good girl," he teased gently.

"So did I," she retorted, smiling back at him. "And I am, normally. You bring these things out in me."

Like lightning he rolled her over, pinning her beneath him. "I hope I do," he said, looking down at her, loving the way her cheeks flushed and her eyes widened and her breath started to come in little gasps. "I look at you when you're trying to be all prim and proper and I have to get under your skin. It's a compulsion."

"An extremely childish compulsion," she said, trying to speak sternly. "Also, you agreed we would not be having sex again tonight."

"Who's having sex?" he said innocently. He lowered himself enough so she could feel his erection between her thighs. "I'm just lying here."

"Well, cut it out," she said, pushing at his chest, and he moved away immediately, lying back down on his side to face her.

"Sorry," he said ruefully. "It really is hard for me not to get carried away around you."

She laid a palm against his chest. "I need a little time before that happens again," she said, and her voice was almost pleading. "Maybe it's hard for you to understand, but I need a chance to…to process. That's just how I am. Take it or leave it."

"I'll take it," he said immediately, knowing it wasn't the offer he was looking for but willing to wait. Then he held out his arms.

She hesitated a moment and then scooted over so she was nestled against him, and he wrapped his arms around her as if she belonged there.

Which she did, Alex thought as he reached across her to turn out the light.

Now all he had to do was convince Holly of that.

Chapter Nine

It was morning. Holly knew this because she could feel warm sunlight against her eyelids.

She knew something else, too. It was hovering just out of reach, some fact of immense significance, something with consequences.

She opened her eyes and saw Alex lying on his side, facing her, a foot of space between them. The blankets covered him to the waist but he was unmistakably naked. He was also awake.

"Hi," he said, smiling. In the morning light the crinkles at the corners of his eyes were easily visible, and his irises were the color of the sky.

"Oh, my God," Holly said in dawning horror. She sat bolt upright in bed, but that reminded her of the fact that she, too, was naked. She snatched at the top quilt to cover herself.

Alex continued to lie beside her, one arm pillowed under his head. "You know, that's really a pointless gesture. I've been watching you sleep for an hour. I know what you look like naked."

Holly gave him a look as she slid out of bed, taking the quilt with her. "I'm sure you do," she said with dignity.

Alex looked at her in exasperation. "You can't seriously—" He stopped himself, shaking his head. "No, I'm not going to bother." He sighed and rolled onto his back. "It's my fault, really," he said to the ceiling. "I was the one who said we should save it till the morning."

"Save what?" she asked suspiciously.

"This. The big dramatic scene where you hit the ground running and we forget this ever happened." He turned his head to face her. "Only this time I'm not playing. I'm not going to lie or pretend, just to make things easier for you. I want us to be together, Holly. I want to see where this is going. If you don't want that, fine. But I'd at least like to know why. I'll respect any decision you make. I just want to understand why you're making it."

Holly replayed Alex's words in her head, trying to focus.

"That's fair," she said after a moment. "That's certainly fair." She knew she sounded like a lawyer negotiating a settlement, but she couldn't help that. She was torn right now between acute embarrassment and the desire to go back to that bed and beg Alex to make love to her again. Her thought processes were not at their best. She took a breath and spoke again. "I just want you to know…I'm not running away. Not necessarily, anyway. I just—"

"Need some time to think," Alex finished for her, clasping his hands behind his head.

"Yes. I do." She bit her lip as she looked at him, his bare torso unbelievably gorgeous in the golden sunlight that streaked across the bed, a blanket draped across his hips and just barely covering his…

She put a cool hand to her hot cheek. "Cold shower," she said. "For me. Now. Then I'm going to the gym to work off some tension."

He grinned evilly. "There are other ways to—"

She held up a palm. "Don't bother finishing that sentence. I plan to carefully consider all the ramifications of our current situation without having my brain muddled by you."

"Do you always approach your romantic relations like investment planning?"

She continued as if he hadn't spoken. "After I shower, during which time you will go back to your own room, I am getting dressed and going to the gym. Then I'm going out to lunch, somewhere far from you and your body, which is screwing up my mental processes."

"Who told you your mental processes were that hot to begin with?" he asked, grinning.

Holly chose to ignore him as she headed resolutely for the bathroom, her quilt trailing behind her like the robes of an empress. She could hear Alex chuckling from across the room until she slammed the bathroom door shut behind her.

Holly had never worked out so hard in her life. Her inner turmoil translated into raw adrenaline, and she went through her usual circuit with single-minded intensity. When she finished with the Nautilus machines and went over to the stationary bicycles, she was surprised to find Gina on one, pedaling away as if her life depended on it. Holly put a hand on her shoulder and she jumped.

"Holly! Don't sneak up on me like that."

"Gina, what in the world are you doing here? Aren't you flying to Vegas tonight to get married?"

"Well, yes," Gina acknowledged, wiping the back of her neck with a towel. "That's why I'm here."

Holly frowned at her friend. "I'm not following you."

Gina sighed. "I'm scared out of my mind. The only thing that makes me feel better is this, so here I am. It's almost a shame the wedding's tomorrow morning. I'm on my way to having the thighs of Lance Armstrong. I could enter the Tour de France."

Holly pulled her off the bike and marched her over to the juice bar. Sitting Gina firmly down on one of the stools, she ordered two Energy Smoothies and sat down herself.

"Okay, start talking," she said sternly. "What are you afraid of? You're crazy about Henry. You guys are perfect together. You can't wait to marry him."

"True. All true."

"Well, then. What are you scared of?"

Gina rested her elbows on the counter and put her chin in her hands. "Everything. Nothing. Just the idea of being married, I guess."

"You're not going to…" She let it trail off, not certain exactly what she thought Gina might do.

Gina kept her chin in her hands but turned to look at her friend. "Run away? Leave him at the altar? No way. I love Henry, and, anyway, I don't let my fears make my decisions for me."

Holly winced at that, remembering what Alex had said to her last night. "Well, good," she said. "But I still don't get what you're afraid of. I would have thought you'd be, I don't know, radiant."

Gina looked at her in disbelief. "You've never heard of wedding jitters? If I'm feeling this freaked out, I can't even imagine what Henry's going through. His best man is probably talking him down from the ceiling."

Holly thought about it. "I guess I thought wedding jitters are for when you have doubts. And it doesn't sound like you have doubts."

Gina shook her head, exasperated. "I don't have doubts. I love Henry. That's what's so scary. Haven't you ever felt something for a man that knocked you on your butt and scared the pants off you?"

"Yes," Holly answered miserably, causing Gina to jerk upright and almost knock her smoothie onto the floor.

"What! You have not. That was a rhetorical question. I've never seen you messed up over a guy. Who is he? Details, Holly. It's your duty to distract me from my gut-twisting turmoil by telling me about yours."

Holly played with her straw. "It's Alex," she said reluctantly.

She stared at Holly in delighted amazement. "Your son's coach, right? The guy you're staying with now? The guy who carried you out of the Bengal Bar?"

"That would be him."

Gina sat back in satisfaction. "I am really, really going to enjoy this. Tell me all."

Holly started to brush it off, to change the subject like she usually did when her personal life came up. But then she remembered last night, and closed her eyes, and realized that this time, for once, she really did need to talk to someone.

"You remember him, right? From the bar? He's got this body…"

"Believe me, I remember. I wanted to start at his toes and nibble my way up."

"Well, living in the same house with him has not been easy. It was really only Will's being there that kept me sane. And when he went away this weekend—"

"Will took off? Left you and Alex alone together?"

"Yes."

Gina smiled. "Smart kid."

Holly's eyes widened. "You don't think—oh, my God, you don't think he did that on purpose? Trying to push us together or something?"

"I hope so. I've always had a lot of respect for Will's brains."

Holly shook her head quickly. "No. I'm sure Will wouldn't do that. But the fact is, the very first night we were alone together…"

Gina leaned forward, eyes sparkling. "Take your time with the play-by-play here."

Holly sighed. "It was incredible. We were coming in from the rainstorm—you remember how it poured last night. And we—we barely made it inside. We had sex in the front hallway. On the floor."

Gina blinked. "Seriously?"

"Seriously."

"Well, this is a side of you we need to encourage. Good for Alex."

"You have no idea. I never felt anything that intense before. It was…" Her hands moved in the air as she searched for words.

Gina nodded. "You've gone nonverbal, which can be

translated as off-the-scale fantastic. But this is good, right? I don't understand where the angst comes in."

Holly slumped. "The sex was great, and the friendship part is great, too, but I don't think Alex is boyfriend material."

Gina looked at her in disgust. "What is *wrong* with you? Who cares if he's boyfriend material? Just enjoy yourself, Holly. Have some fun. You've earned it. You've spent fifteen years being responsible and competent and a mom and a financial planner. Why don't you enjoy being a woman for a change?"

The thought was so tempting Holly had a sip of smoothie to settle the butterflies in her stomach. "I can't do that," she said finally.

Gina threw up her hands. "Give me one good reason."

"Will."

"Right. Will. Tell me, Holly, how do you think Will would feel if he knew you were using him as an excuse not to be happy?"

"That's not what I'm doing," Holly argued. "It's just…I can't have a wild affair with his coach. Alex is important to Will. They've…they've bonded."

"You're important to Will, too. Why do you think he left this weekend?"

"If, and this is a big if, but *if* Will did leave because he was playing matchmaker or something, then it's even worse. What if he gets his hopes up? How will he feel if—I mean, *when* things don't work out? He'll be devastated. He's already been abandoned by his father. He doesn't need to be disappointed like that again."

"Will's not a little boy, you know. He's a young man."

"He can still be hurt."

Gina looked at her thoughtfully. "Are you sure it's Will you're really worried about? You can be hurt, too, Holly."

"I can take care of myself," she snapped.

Gina raised her eyebrows. "Right, of course. I forgot for a minute who I was talking to. Holly Stanton, the woman who doesn't need help from anyone."

Holly frowned at her. "You're starting to sound like Alex."

Gina sighed. "Look, Holly, it's your life. You need to make your own decisions. I just think that you could have some fun with Alex without causing undue devastation in Will's life or yours. Men *can* be fun, you know."

"Not in my experience," Holly muttered.

"Exactly my point. You need some new experiences. But go ahead, turn your back on some really amazing sex. God forbid you actually let down your guard for two seconds and enjoy yourself."

"Hey! I enjoy myself plenty. With or without the sex."

Gina hopped down from her stool. "I give up. You're hopeless. Let's go pedal ourselves into oblivion."

Holly sighed in relief. "Finally a suggestion that makes sense. Lead the way."

Alex had no idea what to expect when he saw Holly again. He kept busy so he wouldn't think about it too much, gathering up the cleaning products Holly had brought into the house and taking them upstairs to his bedroom, wanting to bring some of her warmth, her magic, into the one place she hadn't been yet.

After he did the floors and the furniture he stripped his bed and took the sheets down to the laundry room.

Holly had bought a new kind of detergent and a box of dryer sheets. An hour and a half later, pulling his bedding from the dryer, he buried his face in the clean scented warmth and felt an ache starting in his heart and spreading to every part of him.

He was upstairs making his bed when he heard the front door open.

"Alex?" Holly called out, her voice tentative, unsure, and Alex went to the head of the stairs and looked down at her.

"Hey," he said.

She held up a red-and-white bucket. "I brought chicken," she said, and he grinned in sudden relief.

"I knew you were my kind of woman," he said, but without a leer or even an eyebrow wriggle, and she grinned back at him.

"Didn't you notice that it's getting dark?" she asked as he came downstairs. "I wasn't sure you were home when I got back, even though I saw your car. There aren't any lights on." She was flicking switches as she spoke, in the hallway and in the living room, where she set the bucket on the coffee table. Alex sat down on the couch, blinking at the pools of mellow light that came on where she went, marveling at the way she illuminated everything she touched.

"Sorry," he said. "How was your day?" he asked, carefully keeping to his side of the sofa when she sat down on the other end.

"It was good," she said, laying out paper plates and plastic silverware. Alex waited for a minute, wondering if she was going to say anything else. When she didn't, he frowned.

"Okay," he said. "I'm trying to let you set the pace

here, but I may need some help with the ground rules. Are we allowed to talk about what happened last night, or—"

"Not yet," Holly said quickly. "Please? Just give me one more night. We'll talk tomorrow, I promise. For tonight I was sort of hoping we could eat greasy takeout and watch a movie or something. If that's okay with you?"

One more night. Well, at least she wasn't rejecting him. Not yet.

"Of course it's okay. What do you want to watch?"

"I rented *The Replacements*."

He raised his eyebrows. "That's a football movie."

"Well, of course. It's football season."

"So it is," Alex said, and settled down to eating chicken and mashed potatoes and keeping his eyes on the television screen instead of Holly's curves.

All things considered, it wasn't too hard. They watched the movie together and then, before there was a chance for things to get awkward, they each said good-night and went to their respective corners. Or in this case, their bedrooms.

Now it was hard. In more ways than one, Alex thought wryly, thinking it was a shame that his innuendoes were wasted on the inside of his head.

Was this going to be his life from now on? Lying awake every night thinking about Holly?

Alex sighed. Maybe he'd be better off if he hadn't seen Holly again, or better yet, had never met her. Now that they'd actually made love it was a thousand times worse. He'd set out to ruin her for all other men and instead she'd ruined him.

Suddenly he threw the covers off and swung his legs over the side of the bed. He needed to get out of this damn house. Take a walk or something. He threw on a pair of jeans and a T-shirt and went into the hallway, noticing that there was a strip of light under Holly's door, which didn't help his peace of mind. He averted his eyes as he went downstairs, where he pulled on a pair of boots and his black leather jacket.

The air outside was cool, and a few thin clouds raced each other across the moon. Alex thrust his hands into his pockets and trudged off on the walk that was somehow going to restore his sanity.

Fat chance.

Holly thought she heard a door slam. She blinked at the book she was holding in her hands, realizing that she'd been staring at the same page for twenty minutes.

Oh, what was the use? She threw the book down on the bed beside her and stared up at the ceiling.

Maybe Gina was right. Did it make sense to burn for someone like this and not have him? Right now it didn't seem to make any sense at all. She was one breath away from getting out of bed and going across the hall to Alex's room.

In fact, she was one breath past it. Holly sat up in sudden determination. She was wearing reasonably nice pajamas, plain and tailored but made of silk, with a camisole top.

Trying very hard not to think too much, or to do anything that would lessen the chances that she would be kissing Alex within the next two minutes, Holly slipped out of bed and tiptoed across the room, hesitating just a moment before opening her door. A moment after that she was standing in his doorway.

He wasn't there.

She remembered the slamming door she'd heard and sighed in frustration. He'd gone for a walk. To cool down, probably. He'd been just as hot as she was, and he'd gotten out of the house so he wouldn't act on it. Great. He was doing exactly what she'd asked him to. Wonderful.

Kicking herself for having waited this long, Holly went back to her room, crawled into bed and turned out the light. It was for the best, she told herself grimly as moonlight glimmered through the black-lace branches of the tree outside her window. She'd been saved from making a very stupid decision. Tomorrow she and Alex would talk, and decide to do the sensible thing, and in the afternoon Will would be back and everything would return to normal.

It was just too bad for her if normal didn't seem appealing anymore.

She must have fallen asleep eventually, or at least dozed off, because when she opened her eyes and saw Alex standing at her bedside, dappled in shadows and moonlight, she thought at first she was dreaming. He was dressed for the outdoors in his boots and leather jacket, and he smelled like cold night air and autumn leaves.

"Alex?" she said, blinking up at him.

"I'm sorry," he said quickly. "I thought you might still be awake. I thought—" Suddenly he stopped talking and dropped to his knees beside her. "I'm sorry I came in here. But I can't... Knowing you're so close and that I can't have you... I don't think I can do this, Holly. I don't know what to do. Help me out here. Tell me something to make this stop. Tell me you hate me. Tell me to go."

Holly was on her side, facing him. She reached out a hand and stroked the hair off his face. His eyes, which had closed, opened wide at her touch. "I can't," she whispered. "I don't know what I want, either, but I don't want you to go. Why is it so much easier to tell the truth at night?"

Alex captured the hand that was stroking his hair, placing a butterfly kiss on her palm. It made her shiver. "I don't know," he said, looking at her. "But I wish the sun would never come up again."

For a moment they stayed like that, and the silence was so deep and rich that Holly could hear both of them breathing, and the whisper of the leaves outside her window. And then Alex's hands were on her bare arms, his palms ghosting over her skin, raising goose bumps everywhere he touched.

Holly felt suddenly shy and scooted away, at least as far as the headboard. Alex only smiled, grasping her wrists and pinning them against her pillow as he climbed on top of her, his knees on either side of her hips. He still had his boots and his jacket on, and fully dressed like this he was somehow so masculine, so possessive, that all she could do was wait, heart pounding, for what he would do next.

The covers were down by her hips, and Holly watched as Alex's eyes roved lazily over her flat stomach. She was shiveringly aware that her camisole had ridden up above her belly button. Her muscles tightened, as if she'd stepped into icy water.

Then his gaze moved up to her breasts, and Holly felt her body responding as if his look were a touch. A shudder passed through her and her nipples hardened, and she could only watch him watching it happen, and see the smile that crossed his face.

"You're evil," she whispered, and he exerted a little

more pressure on her wrists, pinning them firmly before he released her suddenly, straightening up and laying a palm on her belly above the waistband of her pajama bottoms. Holly could have sworn her body hummed and vibrated at the touch of his cool hand against her hot skin. Then his hand was moving, sliding under the hem of her camisole, over her ribs, and then—oh, *yes*— covering her right breast.

Holly couldn't help herself. She arched her back, needing to feel more, needing something—

Alex seemed to know exactly what she needed. His other hand moved to cover her left breast and his thumbs were working some kind of magic across her nipples, sending bolts of pleasure straight to her core.

Any tiny bit of resistance she might have clung to melted like butter in the sun as Holly let out a wordless cry of pleasure.

His hands were moving again, tugging off her top, and she raised herself up enough to help him before she sank back down on the bed and Alex lowered his head, taking one breast in his mouth while his hand caressed the other. When he grazed his teeth across the hyper-sensitive flesh she gasped, and when he blew cool breath across her wet skin she moaned.

She was so saturated with desire it took her a few seconds to notice he was kissing his way down her stomach, and then lower.

She tensed up and put a hand in his hair to stop him.

He looked up at her, and seemed to know right away that she was a little nervous about what he was about to do.

"Trust me, Holly," was all he said.

Then he hooked his thumbs in the waistband of her

pajama bottoms, catching her panties too, and in two seconds they were gone, a satin puddle on the floor, and she was completely exposed to him.

"You're the most beautiful woman I've ever seen," Alex said softly, his blue eyes almost black in the moonlight, and then he slid his hands between her knees and exerted steady, irresistible pressure, and Holly let her legs fall open so Alex could move between them, his leather jacket smooth and cool against her thighs and his hands coming to rest on her bare hips.

For a moment he was still, just looking at her. The sight of him like that, fully dressed and cherishing her, was so much sexier than anything she'd ever experienced that she felt a rush of moisture at her center. She gasped when he pressed his thumbs into her soft flesh and opened her gently. Then he lowered his head and licked her, flicking his tongue across the heart of her.

Her need for him was a riptide in her body, pulling and pushing at the same time. She was shaking uncontrollably now, a storm building, rocking her, and he had to stop but he should never stop, never stop, never, never—

When the storm burst she cried out, bucking against him, and his hands and mouth stayed on her, gentler now, riding out the waves until she began to still, and then he moved to cover her body with his, and the sensation of his jeans and leather jacket against her naked, sensitized skin almost made her come again.

She took deep, deep breaths as he licked the sweat from her throat and between her breasts, and then she had her hands in his hair and was tugging him upward.

She pulled him to her, and then it was mouth on mouth and tongues exploring softly, almost shyly, and she could taste the tang of herself for a moment but then it was all Alex, the wild heat of Alex, surrounding her and penetrating her and making her feel more glorious things than she'd ever felt in her life.

Alex broke their kiss and looked down at her, and saw her eyes drifting closed. He levered himself up and off the bed, pulling the covers up to tuck Holly in, and then kneeling down by her pillow. He was distracted by the look on her face, an expression of completely satisfied desire. He couldn't stop himself from lowering his head to taste her lips one more time.

After a long, soft kiss he pulled away, stroking her hair away from her face, loving the way the flush of pleasure lingered in her cheeks.

Her eyes fluttered closed again.

"Go to sleep," he said gently. "I'll go back to my room to give you your space."

"But...nothing happened for you," she murmured, her cheek pillowed on her hand.

Alex smiled. "Don't worry about me. You're tired, and I think you might feel better tomorrow morning if you wake up alone. Less pressure. We do still have to talk, you know."

She nodded, and Alex dropped one last kiss on her forehead before rising to his feet and backing away. "Good night, Holly. Sleep well."

She was drifting off as he closed the door behind him.

He took a quick shower to calm his body down and crawled naked into bed, his hair still damp. He felt at peace for the first time all day as he closed his eyes and fell asleep.

* * *

Holly woke up feeling better than she ever had in her life. Her eyes were clear, blinking in the morning light—by the angle it couldn't be much after dawn—and her mind was clear, too.

Remembering the events of last night, she closed her eyes and made a little sound at the back of her throat.

She opened her eyes suddenly. She wanted to make Alex feel that way, and for the first time in her life, she thought she could. Holly had never felt very sure of herself in bed, never sure about the pleasure she was giving or receiving, but a confidence was rushing through her now, not that she knew what to do but that she'd be able to figure it out. If she wasn't sure, she could ask Alex to tell her. He was so passionate, so uninhibited, that he made her feel that way, too.

Luckily she was still naked.

This time, standing in his doorway, she was glad to see Alex in bed, sound asleep on his back with one arm flung out to the side. She went over to him softly, taking hold of his covers and pulling them down slowly and carefully, smiling when she saw that he, too, hadn't bothered with clothes last night.

She climbed onto the bed and lay down beside him, farther down than he was, and took him softly in her hand.

Then his hands were in her hair and he was saying *"Holly?"* as if he could hardly believe what was happening.

She stopped what she was doing to smile up at him. "Hi," she said.

"What are you *doing?*"

"Reciprocating," she said.

She heard him moan, felt him tense, and suddenly he sat up, pulling her into his lap and kissing her fiercely.

Then the kiss stopped and Alex slid off the bed. "Wait here," he ordered her, stabbing a finger in her direction and heading out the door. She heard him go down the stairs, and a minute later he was coming up them again.

"What in the world are you doing?" she asked as he came back into the room carrying a portable CD player.

"Fulfilling a fantasy," he said with a grin, setting the stereo down on the dresser and hitting the play button. A moment later Marvin Gaye was singing "Let's Get It On" and Alex was coming toward her, wearing the sexiest smile Holly had ever seen.

"I love this song," she said.

"It makes me think about you. About making love to you." He sat down on the bed next to her, stroking his hand down her naked shoulder.

She shivered at his touch. "I never figured you for the romantic type," she said.

"I'm not, normally. You bring it out in me." He leaned over to kiss her and she slid her hand down his body to cup him in her hand.

Alex froze against her briefly, sucking in air.

"I want you," he said roughly. "I want to be inside you. Do you want that?"

"Yes," she breathed.

His hand tightened on her shoulder for one moment. Then he pulled back to open the drawer of his nightstand for a condom.

He opened the little foil packet but then she took it from him, taking her time sliding the lubricated latex over his arousal, smiling when she heard him catch his breath.

"Red-haired witch," he said, pulling her closer so that she was straddling him, and then using his hands to guide her down on top of him.

As she slid down his hard length she felt his hands on her hips tense, gripping her hard. A shiver ran through her at the feel of that hard masculinity inside her, all that raw power beneath her, and at the glorious freedom of being the one on top, able to set the pace.

She leaned forward, putting her hands flat on his chest, and watched his face as she began to move, finding a rhythm that made his eyes close and his head rock back, the strong, corded muscles of his neck tensing and releasing as he clenched his jaw.

She was so distracted by the passion and intensity in his face that she didn't notice how close she was to her own release. Then she felt the tremors beginning, in her fingers and toes this time, and then traveling like white lightning to her core. She exploded, crying out and tightening all her muscles, including some she hadn't known she possessed, and Alex was first rigid beneath her and then pulsing inside of her as he called her name and opened his eyes to meet hers for one blinding moment.

Once again it was a while before they could move or speak. Eventually Alex dislodged her gently and then slid down to lie beside her, trailing a hand along the perfect curve that dipped from her torso to her waist and then up to her hip.

"I think you broke me this time," she said, her face turned into the pillow and her voice muffled.

He chuckled. "If that's true it's only fair for me to fix you. Let's see, how could I manage that?"

Without opening her eyes Holly scooted so that she was cuddled against his chest, the top of her head tucked under his chin and her arm around his waist. Alex felt a stirring of something, a feeling that was probably as old as time. It was a voice inside him that said, "This is my woman, and I'll look after her until the day I die."

He held her tight, and she nestled closer, and he reached up to pull the covers over them both.

And within minutes they were asleep.

Chapter Ten

"Hello! Are you guys here? I'm home!"

Alex's eyes flew open, but Holly was faster. She sprang out of bed, looking around wildly and grabbing a towel off his floor to cover herself with.

"Oh, my God, it's Will. Alex, you have to get down there so I can get back to my room and change. Throw some clothes on, anything."

Alex's head was still fuzzy with sleep but he heard the urgency in Holly's voice and he moved as quickly as he could. As he was heading out the door in sweats and a T-shirt Holly grabbed his arm. "I'll be down in a minute," she hissed at him. "Don't say anything about—about this."

Her words echoed in his head as he went down the stairs to greet Will. Did she mean don't say anything ever, or that she wanted to be the one to tell him? Now is not the time to worry about that, he told himself as he arrived at the bottom of the stairs and looked around for Will. He and Holly still had to talk, that was all. But she wouldn't turn her back on the feeling that was obviously between them. Not after this morning. Would she?

Alex found Will in the kitchen, opening a cooler that contained ice and three smallish trout.

"Look!" Will said enthusiastically, and in spite of the disorientation of having woken up two minutes before and his nagging anxiety about Holly, Alex couldn't help grinning at the happy teenager. "Will, that's great. Where are the rest of them?"

"This is it," Will said, looking down at his catch with pride. "From this morning, anyway. We caught some yesterday, but we ate them."

"Of course," Alex said, holding back a smile. "Out of the water and onto your plate. It's the only way to go."

"You bet. So—" He turned to Alex with a speculative look. "How was *your* weekend? Did you have any fun?"

It was either his imagination, or Will knew something. Or suspected something. Or—

"Will, did you go away this weekend on purpose?"

He looked guilty, which confirmed it. "What do you mean, on purpose?"

"You know what I mean." He turned his head as he heard Holly coming down the stairs, and he had time to say, "Don't say anything to your mom, not one word," before she came into the kitchen, smiling brightly. She was wearing corduroys and a dark green sweater, and her hair was caught back in a pony tail.

"Hi, honey! You're back early!"

"I am? I said Sunday afternoon, didn't I?" he said, looking confused. Alex followed Holly's eyes to the clock, which read 2:00 p.m.

"Oh. Right." She took a breath. "Well, good for you. Punctuality is important. Very, very important. So how was…how was your…" Her eyes drifted to the cooler, and her eyebrows rose. "A veritable feast, I see," she said gravely, sounding more like herself, and Alex breathed a sigh of relief.

"Mr. Washington said I did very well for a beginner. Of course he and Tom caught about twenty apiece, and they offered to give me some of theirs to take home, but I said I just wanted to take the ones I caught myself. So you could see them."

Holly went over and gave her son a quick hug. "I agree with Mr. Washington. I think you did great. I assume this is going to be our next meal?"

"If that's okay with you guys," Will said anxiously.

"Of course it is," Holly said. "I'll be happy to cook them, unless you want to. I will *not* clean them, however. That job is all yours."

"No problem," Will said proudly. "Tom taught me how."

"Wonderful. We may as well get started now, unless you've already eaten. Alex and I haven't had lunch yet—" She blushed, although Alex noticed she didn't look at him "—so we're starving."

"Sounds good," Will said. "I haven't had anything since breakfast."

Despite a little awkwardness in the air, their late lunch was fun, not to mention delicious. Alex felt himself relaxing as Will regaled them with his fishing triumphs, and he saw that Holly was unwinding, too.

It was toward the end of the meal that it hit him.

Will was laughing so hard at something Holly said that he got the hiccups, and Holly found that so funny she couldn't stop laughing, either. She'd start to say something, but then Will would hiccup, and that would start her laughing again. Will was drinking water in an effort to stop when *Holly* started hiccupping, and Will found that so hilarious he sprayed a mouthful of water all over the table.

That was when it hit him. Some of the water hit him, too, which both mother and son found extremely amusing. But the important thing, the big thing, was the realization.

He loved them.

He thought it exactly like that. *I love them.* Not just *I love her,* but *I love them.* Because what he wanted was the whole package. Holly and Will, part of his life forever.

Forever.

The knowledge felt huge, as if he wasn't big enough to hold it. He couldn't stay still. He rose to his feet.

Holly and Will looked up at him. Will was still hiccupping, but Holly had stopped. "Are you okay? You have the strangest look on your face."

"I—"

He couldn't say it. Not yet, anyway. He'd never said it to anyone before. What was the procedure? Did you just blurt it right out, or what? Should he tell Holly alone, or both of them together?

He needed some time to think. To get his thoughts in order.

Air, he thought. He needed some air.

"I'll be right back," he said, crossing the kitchen and going out the back door.

* * *

"Is Alex okay? I didn't mean to spit on him," Will said after he finally controlled his hiccups.

Holly grinned. "I'm pretty sure he knows that." The phone rang, and Holly went to go answer it. "Clear the table, would you?" she called over her shoulder as she went into the living room.

"Hello?"

"Oh…hello. Is Alex there?"

A female voice, breathy and hopeful. Holly rolled her eyes. "He's just stepped outside. Can I take a message, or do you want me to call him?"

"Um…I guess you can take a message. Tell him Krystal called. Krystal with a K," she added helpfully.

Of course, Holly thought as she wrote down the name. It was important to be specific with Alex, because he'd probably dated a girl named Crystal with a C, too.

"Does he have your number?"

"It's changed, actually. Can I give you the new one?"

"You bet." Holly made a face at the phone as she wrote the number down beside the name.

She was still staring down at the piece of paper when Alex came into the living room.

"Message for you," she said, handing it to him. He put it in his pocket without looking at it.

"Holly, I—"

"Don't you want to know who called?"

He still looked funny. "Not particularly. Look, Holly, can we talk somewhere in private? Maybe over dinner or a drink or—"

"It was Krystal."

He blinked. "Crystal?"

"The woman who called. Her name was Krystal."

"The woman who called."

"Uh-huh. Krystal with a K."

He frowned at her. "Holly, is something wrong?"

"No, nothing at all. So tell me about Krystal. Did she come before or after Amber?"

Just listen to her. She was talking like a jealous girlfriend.

He was looking down at her with one eyebrow raised. "Did you think I was lying when I told you I'm not seeing anybody? When I told you I have no plans to see anybody? Except for you," he added, and the look in his blue eyes made her stomach flip.

She folded her arms across her chest. "Look, it's none of my business," she said.

"Actually, it is. As the woman I'd like to...date, I think it is your business. I think you have a right to know there isn't anyone else. That there won't be anyone else."

God, those eyes. It was hard to think straight when he was looking at her like that, as if she was the only woman in the world.

He wanted to date her? As in...exclusively?

She wanted to believe it. She was surprised at how much she wanted to believe it. Maybe *he* even believed it, for now. But Alex was not a long-haul guy. And how would Will deal with the fallout when they broke up?

How would *she* deal with it?

"Let's go out for a drink," he was saying now. "How about the Swan?"

The Swan was a pub downtown, known for its intimate atmosphere and dark, tryst-inducing booths.

"No," she said quickly. "Look, Alex...I know we still haven't talked about...about what happened between us. But Will just got back, and I…I need a little time with him. And a little time to myself, too. Is it okay if we talk tomorrow?"

He looked as if he wanted to press the point, but after a moment he sighed.

"We can talk tomorrow," he said. His eyes were still on her, with the focused intensity that made her pulse go all skittery. "But you can't hide forever, Holly Stanton."

Didn't she know it.

She didn't want to be this person. She'd structured her life so she *wouldn't* be this person. This person who could be thrown into a jealous fit after one phone call, this person whose heartstrings and nerve endings now seemed to be tuned to Alex—his voice, his smile, his eyes.

She'd sworn that her happiness would never again depend on another human being. Now here she was, unreasonably jealous one minute, melting with affection and desire the next. And all because of Alex.

It was after midnight, and everyone else was asleep. Holly was pacing back and forth in her room. No, not her room—Alex's room. In Alex's house. After her parents kicked her out, she'd sworn to herself she'd never live even a day in a place that wasn't her own. A place someone else could kick her out of.

Not that Alex would—but he could. Anytime he wanted to, he could.

She opened her door and moved softly down the hall, pausing a moment outside Alex's door.

She closed her eyes, memories of their lovemaking making her shiver. Alex had ignited her, body and mind and heart and soul, and the heat between them had burned away all barriers until she hadn't known where he ended and she began.

And that might be a nice way to feel in bed with someone, but then you had to get out of bed and on with your life. And that's when the feeling became terrifying. Holly was used to knowing exactly where she ended and other people began. Feeling this…*connected* to someone just wasn't something she'd ever signed up for.

She forced herself to start walking again, down the hall and down the stairs. Once on the first floor she turned on a few lights, enough to see her way as she wandered from room to room of the house she'd grown so comfortable in.

She felt connected to Will, of course, but that wasn't the same thing. She was the mom, so her job was to be in control, to be responsible. With Alex, she felt… carried away. Out of control. Her feelings for Alex were growing faster than she could analyze them, and already they seemed somehow exponentially beyond analysis, as if she were trying to use a microscope to study the sun.

Being that connected to someone meant pain if they left. Feelings of helplessness, loneliness and neediness. Feelings Holly had sworn she'd never go through again.

She'd walked through every room downstairs and now she paused in the front hallway, turning on the light switch, the soft glow from the old-fashioned chandelier reminding her of Friday night and the way Alex had talked to her, challenged her, forced her outside her defenses.

She turned the light off again and went back into the living room.

It was too much. Being with Alex had opened up

wells of feeling within her, and she didn't want to know what was at the bottom. She tried to imagine what she would feel if—no, make that *when*—Alex left her.

Not because he was a bad guy. Not because he didn't care about her. But because it wasn't his nature to tie himself to one woman, and because experience had taught her that it was in few men's natures to be tied down to a single mother.

And let's say he gave it the old college try. Let's say everything seemed to be going along just fine. Experience had taught her something about that, too—when you let yourself be comfortable, let yourself relax, then something would happen to knock you flat.

But none of those fears even came close to the fear of Will getting hurt. He'd already been abandoned by his father... He didn't need to lose a father figure, too. Not one he liked as much as Alex.

Holly picked up a wooden statue from the top of a bookcase, a carved giraffe that a former player had given Alex. Her fingers caressed it before she set it back down. And then she realized what she'd been doing for the last hour, going from room to room of Alex's house, touching the things she associated with him.

She was saying goodbye.

The next morning, after Will and Alex had both left for the day, Holly called in to work and took a personal day. Then she went out to her favorite coffee shop and bought a morning paper.

There were a few likely ads in the real-estate section, both apartments and houses for rent, but the problem was Holly didn't feel like taking the time to look around and make a careful decision, or waiting for the first of the month to move in.

She glanced at the clock on the wall. Eleven o'clock in the morning. Eight o'clock in Vegas, which was way too early to call a woman on her honeymoon. Holly did some window-shopping in town and had a light lunch, and forced herself to wait until one—ten in the morning Vegas time—before she called Gina's cell phone.

Her voice, when it came, sounded sleepy but very happy. "Good morning, good morning whoever you are, you've reached Mrs. Henry Walthrop!"

In spite of her own worries Holly smiled. "So I take it you didn't run away."

Gina gave a contented sigh. "Nope. And it's a good thing. Married life suits me. Of course being waited on hand and foot in a honeymoon suite may be affecting my judgment." There was a pause and the sound of a wet kiss. "No, on second thought, I think it's all Henry."

"Gina, I'm really happy for you. And I'm sorry to bother you when you're on your honeymoon, but I have a pretty big favor to ask."

"Anything, sweetie. Shoot."

"Your apartment. Is it still available?"

"Absolutely. My lease doesn't run out till the end of the year, so unless I find someone to sublet I'm stuck paying the rent till then."

"Well, you've just found someone to sublet. How soon can I move in?"

Gina hesitated. "Anytime, I guess. The superinten-dent has the keys. All my clothes and things are moved out but it's still furnished, which makes it easy. But what's going on? I thought you guys were sort of settled at Alex's place." A beat went by. "Oh. Okay, I get it. I guess things didn't go so well with Alex, huh? Were you too chicken to go for it when he jumped you?"

"Not exactly." Holly cleared her throat. "The jumping was pretty much mutual. And he said he wants to date me."

"But that's great! Isn't it great?"

"Well…"

"Holly Stanton, give me one good reason why this isn't great."

"Because Alex has never been in a relationship that lasted longer than three months! Because I've never been in a relationship that didn't end with the guy running away from me! First Brian, then Mark—"

"Don't you know there's a first time for everything?"

"Not for this. Not for me."

"Okay, Holly. I'm about to tell you something important, so pay attention. It's time for you to stop surviving and start living. I know Brian was a low-down bastard, and I know your parents let you down. I know you put a wall around your heart to get through those first few years alone. But those days are over. It's not just you and Will against the world anymore."

Holly closed her eyes. "Just tell me whether or not I can have your apartment. I need a place to stay."

"Of course you can have the damn apartment! But when I get back home you and I are going to have a serious discussion."

"Fine. Whatever. I'll buy the drinks." She took a deep breath. "And, Gina? Congratulations."

"On being happy? Thanks, I appreciate it. Want to know my secret? Not being blind *and* stupid enough to let the right guy go."

Holly sighed. "Enjoy the rest of your honeymoon, Gina."

* * *

By the time Will and Alex came home from practice, everything was done. Holly had moved their few possessions to the new place, and washed her and Will's sheets and remade the beds. She made dinner, too, steak and green salad and mashed potatoes. It was waiting on the table when Will and Alex came through the door.

"Hi," she said as cheerfully as she could. She glanced at Alex, who grinned at her before hanging up his jacket, and then at Will who was rubbing the back of his neck.

"Dinner's on the table," she said, wishing her heart wouldn't turn over in her chest every time Alex smiled at her. "Rough day at practice?" she asked her son as they went into the kitchen. Will slumped down into his chair with a groan.

"Say hello to the Wildcats' new starting quarterback," he said. "Apparently Coach's training plan for a rookie QB is to try really hard to kill him, and if it doesn't work, then he's ready for game day."

Holly had stopped in the middle of serving salad. "But…how? I thought with the bye week Charlie would be able to—"

Alex shook his head. "It's an ACL injury. He's out for the season."

Holly finished dishing supper and sat down herself. "But Will's only fifteen," she said to Alex, frowning. "What if he gets hurt like Charlie did?"

"Hey, I'm sitting right here. And if Coach doesn't manage to kill me there is nothing, and I mean nothing, that an opposing team will be able to do to me."

"Who are you playing this week?" she asked.

"The Silverton Warriors," Alex said.

"They'll be a pushover," Will assured her, putting an enormous bite of steak into his mouth.

"Hey," Alex said, smiling at him. "Just because you completed a few passes today is no excuse to get cocky."

"I'm not cocky," Will said with his mouth full. "The Warriors are terrible. Are you trying to tell me they're not terrible?"

Alex rolled his eyes. "Okay, yes, they're terrible. But that still doesn't mean you can be overconfident."

"How much do you want to bet we win this game?"

Alex folded his arms. "You want me to bet against my own team? Ever hear of a guy named Pete Rose?"

"Just a friendly wager, Coach. If we lose Friday's game I'll wash the dishes for a month."

Holly had been listening with half her attention, trying to work up the courage to tell them her news. But now she needed to speak up.

"Actually," she said awkwardly, "the dishes aren't going to be an issue anymore. Will and I are going to be moving out."

Will swallowed a bite of mashed potato. "Sure, eventually. But in the meantime someone has to—"

"Not eventually. It's done. We're moving into Gina's apartment tonight."

Will and Alex both stared at her. After a minute Alex set his fork down on the table. "That was fast," he said evenly.

"What do you mean, tonight?" Will asked, sounding bewildered. "And why? Alex doesn't mind having us here and we—"

"We can't trespass on Alex's hospitality forever," Holly interrupted. "Look, this isn't up for discussion. I told you, it's done. I spoke to Gina and the building superintendent and I moved our things over there today."

Will's fork clattered onto his plate. "I can't believe it," he said. "You've never called out of work in your entire life, but you did today so you could do this behind my back?"

"Behind your back? Will, I'm your mother. I still make the decisions for this family."

"Got it," Will said, pushing his chair violently back from the table. "Of course. Because you always know what's best, right? Well, you know what? You don't know *anything*. I bet you think you're protecting me, too. That's always your excuse when you're actually protecting yourself."

He was on his feet now, his expression angrier than Holly had ever seen it. She could only stare at him with her mouth open. "I'm going next door to say goodbye to Anna," he said stiffly. "I've been helping her with her yard work, and I don't want her to think I've just disappeared on her. Decent people don't do that."

"Will, you can still come by here whenever you—"

"Forget it, Mom. You can try selling it to Alex, but he's pretty smart. I don't think he'll buy it any more than I do."

Will's outburst was so sudden and so out of character that Holly felt tears starting behind her eyes. Determined that Alex wouldn't see her cry, she snatched up her dishes with shaking hands and took them to the sink, where she could stand with her back to the room while she tried to compose herself.

Behind her she could hear Alex's chair scrape against the floor as he got to his feet.

"Is there a chance this doesn't mean you're breaking up with me?"

His voice was cold, and she couldn't look at him. "We were never really together," she said, hearing her own voice tremble. She turned on the water to fill the sink and held her hands under the stream. Her skin felt tight, and there was an ache at the back of her throat.

"I see."

The water was painfully hot, but she didn't move her hands or turn on the cold tap. If only she could burn these feelings away, burn them out of her, make them stop—

"I told you Saturday morning I'd accept any decision you made, as long as I understood why you're making it. At the time, you said that was fair."

She swallowed around the pain. "It is fair," she said. "I just—"

"I'm going out for a run now. When I get back, we're going to talk."

He didn't wait for a response.

She listened to his footsteps as he left the kitchen. Two tears escaped, one from each eye, slipping down her cheeks like rain. Then she took a deep breath and started to wash the dishes.

Chapter Eleven

Alex ran harder and faster than normal, trying to drive out emotion with physical activity. This was a trick he'd gotten pretty good at over the years, from the time he was a little boy dealing with his mother's death by getting into fights with the neighborhood kids.

Football had always been an outlet for him—a source of joy, too. And it was a good thing he still had football in his life, because it didn't look as if he was going to have Holly.

Unless he could convince her to give them a shot.

By the time he got back to the house, the sun was sinking toward the tree-covered hills to the west. He walked slowly across the front lawn, feeling his heart rate slow, using the sleeve of his sweatshirt to wipe the sweat away from his eyes.

"Alex," he heard Holly say, and she was there in

front of him, the red glory of the clouds the perfect backdrop for her fair skin and flaming hair.

She looked young and fragile as she stared up at him, her green eyes anxious. She had such a powerful personality it was easy to forget how small she really was, how slender, her bones as delicate as a child's. She looked like a child right now, in that bulky brown sweater with her hair pulled back in a ponytail.

But she wasn't a child.

"Alex, I—I'm so sorry. I wish things were different."

"Yeah? Different how?"

"I was afraid this would happen. You've been so good to Will and me—you took us in after the fire, made us feel at home. I don't know what we would have done without you. And you and I…we were build-ing a real friendship, a friendship that…that meant so much…and now it's destroyed." Her lower lip trem-bled. "I wish we'd never slept together."

That felt as harsh as any blow he'd ever received on a football field. He stared at her. "How can you wish that? Those nights with you were the best nights of my life. Making love with you was—I don't have words for what it was. And I *know* you were there with me."

She looked away from him. "That's not what I meant," she said miserably. "I didn't mean…of course I feel the same way. About…about those nights. But we'd be crazy to think we could have anything more than that. Just look at our track records."

He took a step closer to her. "You mean my track record. But Holly…the way I feel about you…I've never felt like this about anyone." It was now or never. "Holly, I love you."

She fell back a step, looking stunned. "What did you say?"

"You heard me." He ran a hand through his hair, closing his eyes against the rays of the setting sun. "And I'm guessing from your horrified expression that you're not about to say you love me, too."

"Alex, I—I can't."

"Can't, or won't?"

"I don't know what you mean."

He opened his eyes. "Yes, you do. I know you feel something for me, Holly. Don't you want to give this a chance? To give us a chance?"

She folded her arms across her chest. "Alex, you've never even left a toothbrush at a woman's house. You've always liked playing the field. And now you expect me to believe you'll give that up—give up your freedom? Give it up for a single mom with a teenage son?"

"Yes." He meant it with his whole heart, but Holly didn't look convinced.

He sighed. "Holly, it's true that I've never been in a serious relationship. But did you ever stop to think—"

"What?"

He took in a breath and let it out. "I've wondered about it, too. Why none of the women I've dated ever got under my skin. Why I never seem to meet The One."

He took a step closer. "Maybe the reason I never met The One is that I already have. Maybe the reason no woman can get under my skin is that you're already there. I was always too proud to admit it, even to myself—but I think I've been in love with you for a long time."

The sun dropped behind the hills, bringing dusk, and

the shadows made the air seem colder. Holly shivered, wrapping her arms around herself.

"Alex, you can't really think—why would you say—"

"Holly, I'm just telling you how I feel. I love you, and I love Will, too. I want both of you in my life. Isn't that enough to take a chance on?"

And then he felt Holly withdrawing from him, actually felt it, as if she were physically pulling away.

"You feel that way now, but—Alex, you can't guarantee the future. If we only had ourselves to think about, maybe we could take a chance. But like you said, Will is in this equation, too. I can't take a chance with Will's happiness, not ever. I won't risk him getting hurt."

"He got hurt tonight."

"I know, and it was because of us. He'd get hurt a lot worse if we tried being a couple and things fell apart. If he got attached to you, not just as a coach but as some sort of father figure. I'm sorry, Alex, but I just can't do this."

Her face looked remote, as if she was already gone. And Alex knew he was beaten.

He was still breathing, but the action felt strange, alien. His chest felt empty, as if something important had been taken out.

His skin was clammy with dried sweat. "I need to take a shower," he said, and his voice sounded strange in his own ears.

Holly's lip was trembling again, and his instinct was still to comfort her, to take her in his arms and pull her close.

He forced his hands to stay at his sides. "Good luck at the new place, Holly."

The walk back to his house was the longest he'd ever taken.

* * *

The next few days were bad.

Holly had never felt so stiff and unnatural around her own son. There had never been anything they couldn't talk about before. Then again, she'd never tried to talk to him about anything like this.

She did try, once, when they were eating dinner at the kitchen counter. "Honey, I'm sorry about how sudden all this was. I'm sorry I didn't talk to you beforehand about moving to Gina's. For reasons I'm not comfortable discussing it was really important to me to—"

Will didn't even look up at her. "Yeah, I know. You had to leave because Alex is in love with you and you're totally freaked out. Do you really think I didn't notice, Mom? Or do you think it's none of my business? I'm just your son. You know, the person who cares more about you than anybody in the whole world."

He pushed away from the counter and left the kitchen, going down the hall and into the small second bedroom he had moved into.

Holly stared after him, her mouth open. Then she leaned forward and put her head in her hands. So Will knew. Had Alex told him or had he figured it out on his own? Did it matter? Her own son thought she was cold and unfeeling. Plus he absolutely worshipped Alex. In a million years he'd never understand why she couldn't love his hero.

Well, why couldn't she? Maybe she really was cold and unfeeling. Alex had told her he loved her, and she might as well have spit in his face.

The worst day of all came when she was looking for a CD in the stack Alex had given her, and found one with a homemade cover mixed in with the others.

For Holly—To Take To A Desert Island.

She sat staring at it for a long time, knowing she shouldn't open it, and knowing with even greater certainty that she shouldn't listen to it.

She was alone in the apartment—Will wouldn't be back for an hour. There was no one around to see her cry.

And she did cry, hugging her knees on the living room floor and listening to Bruce Springsteen and Joni Mitchell and Aretha Franklin and Van Morrison. But when Marvin Gaye started singing "Let's Get It On," she turned the CD player off. The pain inside her was like a living thing.

She went to the sink to splash water on her face.

There was no use in crying. It was all over now. It was for the best, she told herself over and over. It was for the best.

If only things with Will could go back to normal.

He did seem to thaw a little toward her the rest of that week. They were talking again, with at least an approximation of their old camaraderie, although Holly suspected that Will was so anxious about his upcoming debut as the Wildcats' starting quarterback that he would have talked to anybody just to relieve the tension.

Holly was surprisingly nervous herself on game night, both for Will's sake—although she'd been careful not to let him know that—and because she'd be seeing Alex for the first time since moving out of his house. Of course there was no reason to expect they'd get within twenty feet of each other, but still she'd be seeing him, and who knew how she'd react to that. Her emotions were a lot more unpredictable than they used to be.

The beautiful fall weather had come to an end during the week, with a cold front from Canada sweeping down to remind them that winter was on the way. Tonight felt bitter, with an icy drizzle coming down from the iron gray sky, but the stands were still packed for the home game. No one in Weston, Ohio wanted to miss a second of the Wildcats' Cinderella season.

Holly found her usual seat in the bleachers, next to David and Angela Washington, and in spite of all her resolutions she immediately looked down toward the sidelines to see if she could catch a glimpse of Alex.

There he was. He was standing facing the field, so all she could see was his back, covered in a thick Wildcats jacket, but it was in that instant that Holly knew the truth.

She loved him.

The moment couldn't have been less romantic. She was sitting on a grooved metal bleacher seat that was like a block of ice, with the cold seeping into her butt through her jeans, and the object of her affections was fifty feet away surrounded by a bunch of teenaged boys in helmets and pads.

But in the moment of her revelation the cold couldn't touch her. She loved him. She loved Alex McKenna.

All that angst, all that inner turmoil, and the truth came and sat down next to her at a damn football game.

She didn't even think about what would happen next. About what she should do now. It didn't seem to matter. The only thing she was aware of right now was the window that had opened in her heart. The feeling was so strong she thought other people must be aware of it, must be able to see it like a blinking neon sign, but all around her the attention was all on the field, where the opposing teams were just lining up for the opening kickoff.

Her eyes were still on Alex. He seemed to be the only person in the world. He was talking to an official, but in the middle of his conversation he twisted his head to look up into the stands, as if he'd heard someone calling his name. He looked straight at her, and their eyes met for just one moment. Holly's breath came faster, and her mouth opened to tell him, *I love you,* but then the whistle blew to start the game, and he had turned back to watch the action on the field.

It didn't matter. There was plenty of time. Holly felt something that was new in her experience: a kind of serenity. She had looked into her heart and hadn't run away from what she saw there, and in that one moment she felt free. She was free.

She took a deep breath and concentrated on what was happening on the football field. Her son was making his debut as the Wildcats' starting quarterback, and she wasn't going to miss a second of it, no matter how many revelations of true love fell out of the sky tonight.

"Isn't this exciting?" Angela screamed in her ear over the shouting of the crowd.

"It is!" Holly shouted back, and the two women settled in to watch their sons and their teammates working together like a well-oiled machine, bonded together by trust and hard work and faith in themselves, all of it given to them by one man, Alex McKenna.

By the middle of the fourth quarter Tom Washington had rushed for over two hundred yards and a touchdown, and Will had completed sixteen of his twenty-three pass attempts, two of them for touchdowns. Holly cheered until her throat was hoarse, and when the last seconds of the game were ticking away, the Wildcats ahead by ten points, she was on her feet with the rest of the crowd when Will threw his last pass of the game, time ran out and the final whistle blew.

Then it happened. One of the Warriors' defensive linebackers, who'd been frustrated all night long, came through the offensive line and smashed Will to the ground with a vicious hit, helmet to helmet. As the furious Wildcat players pulled him off their starting quarterback the crowd fell suddenly silent.

Will Stanton had failed to get up after the illegal play.

For one frozen moment Holly couldn't move. Then she was crashing down through the stands, clumsily, falling the last few feet and getting up again and running, running, until she could kneel down at Will's side.

"The ambulance is on its way," Alex said, and she looked up to see him kneeling beside her, his eyes on Will's face.

Before she could answer the trainers were there with a stretcher, and calm, professional hands were lifting Will onto it and covering him with a blanket. They started walking him off the field, Holly with them, her hand clutching one of Will's in both her own, and by the time they made it to the parking lot the ambulance was there, lights flashing, and then Holly was riding inside it beside her son, her terror hardly lessened by the paramedic's assurance that his heartbeat was strong and steady.

The next hour was a nightmare. They arrived at the hospital and they wouldn't let her go in with Will, and nurses asked her things, and gave her papers to sign, and no one would tell her anything, even when she grabbed one doctor by the sleeve and begged her.

"Just sit down in the waiting room, Mrs. Stanton. As soon as we know anything we'll tell you."

"It's Miss," Holly whispered as she sank down onto a hard plastic chair. "Miss Stanton."

Maybe if she was a Mrs. this wouldn't have happened. If Will had a father. If she hadn't let him play football. If she'd been paying more attention.

She'd been thinking about Alex, falling in love with Alex, and she'd let her guard down, and look what happened. When would she ever learn?

And then Alex was coming through the door, heading right for her, but at that moment the doctor came through another door.

"He's fine," the white coated woman said immediately, and Holly felt weak with relief, the tears she'd been holding back sliding down her cheeks. "He has a mild concussion. We took X-rays and did an MRI and all the usual tests, and he's absolutely fine. We'll keep him overnight for observation, but that's just a precaution. He regained consciousness during the exam, but fell asleep a few minutes ago. That's normal, too. You're welcome to go in and see him, but he'll probably still be asleep. It would be better not to wake him up."

"I won't," Holly said. "I want to see him now."

Will looked terribly young on the hospital bed, with an IV in his arm and some machine beeping on the table next to him. She stood there watching him, breathing when he breathed, for a long time. At some point a nurse came in and said they needed her at the front desk to fill out some more paperwork.

It was while she was doing that, her hand shaking as she tried to manipulate pen on paper, that Alex came up behind her.

"Holly, I'm so sorry."

"It's not your fault," she said without looking at him. "It's mine." She finished the last page and pushed the clipboard across the counter to the medical receptionist. Alex took her arm and turned her gently to face him.

"Holly, there is no way you can blame yourself for this. If it's anyone's fault it's mine. I let Will start that game even though he's only fifteen—"

"He wanted to play. You couldn't have stopped him."

"I could have taken him out before that last series."

"Why? Are you clairvoyant? Did you think that kid was going to hit him after the whistle like that?"

"Of course not, but I—"

Holly shrugged and started to walk away. "I told you, Alex, it's my fault."

"Holly, that's insane! How can you possibly think that?"

"Because it is."

"Holly, listen to me—"

"I have to go back in to Will."

"Holly, wait. Before you go in there and start telling your son how this is all your fault, which is not what he needs to hear right now, take one minute and talk to me."

Holly stopped walking and turned to face him. "Fine," she said, her voice empty of emotion. They were in a quiet corner of the waiting room and Holly sat down on another hard plastic chair. "What do you want me to say?" she asked.

Alex stared at her for a moment and then sank down into the chair beside her.

"Tell me how this is your fault."

Everything in her felt tight, and hard, and hot. "Because I let my guard down." She met his eyes, and focused on him for the first time. "Sitting there in the stands today, I realized that I'm in love with you. And I felt happy. Really happy, like a child feels, without—without reservations. As if everything was beautiful and wonderful and safe." She took a deep breath and pressed her hands together in her lap. "And then look what happened."

Alex leaned toward her. "You think Will got knocked unconscious because you realized you love me? Because you let yourself feel happy for two seconds?"

"Yes!" she said passionately. "This is what happens when you let yourself go. The first time, I got pregnant and my parents kicked me out of the house. The second time, I got drunk and hungover and I let our house burn down. And now this."

Alex was staring at her as if she were speaking a foreign language. Suddenly it seemed very important to make him understand.

"It's like a bargain I made years ago," she said, and although she didn't realize it, her voice was a little higher than usual, like a young girl's. "I can have Will, I can keep him safe, but only if I—if I—you see, if I'm good, nothing bad will happen. If I don't try to be happy, Will can be happy. And then I broke the bargain. I thought about myself, I let myself love you, and—oh, God, Will!"

Alex put one hand on each side of her face, gently. "Holly, that's crazy. If you listened to yourself you'd see that. You're talking like a frightened little girl, not a grown woman. You—"

Suddenly he stopped. "I get it now," he said, half to himself. "I finally get it."

Holly's face was wet with tears again, and she brushed a hand across her eyes. "You get it, huh? What exactly do you get, Alex?"

He sat back and looked at her. "When you got pregnant. You were young and scared…still a kid, really. Your own parents were ashamed of you. You weren't their perfect little girl anymore. You weren't Brian's perfect girlfriend anymore. The baby you hadn't asked for took everything else away. And you took his side, fought for him against the whole world."

He took a breath. "That's one of the thousand reasons I love you, by the way. You gave birth to Will, and loved him and cared for him, and made a life for him without anybody's help. Still, the loss of your old life had to hurt. You're human. But you couldn't blame Will, could you?"

Holly felt sick to her stomach for some reason. "Of course I couldn't! Blame Will? He's the best thing that ever happened to me!"

Alex nodded. "I know. I know he is. You couldn't blame Will—so you blamed yourself. You still do. That's why you're not allowed to be happy. You're still blaming yourself, even for things you have no control over."

Holly breathed in through her nose. "That's crazy," she said tightly.

"I know it is. But it's true. That's the 'bargain' you were talking about. You're punishing yourself for making a mistake when you were eighteen years old. A mistake that led to Will, who you love more than anything in your life. But you're still to blame for being irresponsible, for letting your guard down. You think if you do it again, something else will be taken away. Like Will. Especially Will. So you don't dare let yourself be happy."

Holly's head was pounding. "You're nuts," she spat out. "I'm not going to sit here and listen to this."

"Fine. But you'll have to grow up sometime, Holly. If you want to be a whole person, you'll have to grow up."

"Grow up? Damn it, Alex, I've always been grown up! I was *born* grown up!"

"Not really. Growing up means letting go of the past. Realizing that life is complicated and that people make mistakes. Realizing that bad things happen, and that you can't prevent them by bargaining with your happiness. Growing up means knowing there are no guarantees, and still having the courage to risk your heart."

Alex leaned toward her again, his hands gripping the arms of his chair as if he were trying not to reach out for her. "Not that it would have been such a risk with me. I love you, Holly. I'll never love anyone else."

Holly drew her knees up against her chest, wrapping her arms around her legs as if to protect herself. "But why?" she said. "Why do you love me? I don't understand it. All I've ever done is push you away."

He smiled a little. "Yeah, well, I'm not saying it's been easy. In fact it's been a major pain in the ass. But if you want to know, I'll tell you."

He drew a deep breath. "I love you because you bug me. Because you're the most exasperating woman I've ever known. Because you got under my skin when I was sixteen years old, and worked your way into my heart.

"I love you because you gave Will the gifts you never had. Gifts I never got, either. You were mother and father to him, and put him ahead of everything else, and gave him all the unconditional love and support you never got from your own parents.

"I love you because underneath your mask you're like a force of nature. You make love like that, you know. With passion. With everything you are. I think you could love a man like that, too—if it was the right man. If you let yourself."

He took another breath. "We belong together. I look at you and I know I'm home, because there isn't any other place in the world I want to be."

He stood up. "But I can't keep asking you for something you can't or won't give. I can't keep offering my heart when it's the last thing in the world you want. It hurts too much, Holly."

He looked toward the wing of the hospital where Will was. "If Will wants to see me anytime, day or night, call me and I'll come." And with that he was gone, pushing through the swinging doors that led outside to the parking lot.

For a long time after he left Holly just sat there, unable to move. Finally she struggled to her feet and went down the hall to Will's room, and the sight of him sleeping peacefully was reassuring and terrifying at the same time. Alex's words came back to her, and she knew that he'd been right, right about everything.

Suddenly, without warning, she slid down to the floor and started to cry.

She cried for what seemed like hours, and as the tears kept coming and coming and the sobs racked her body, Holly felt something deep inside her start to release. Something hard, and tight, and poisonous. Something that had been there a long time.

Eventually the tears slowed. And after a while she was quiet again, feeling empty and drained and oddly peaceful.

"Hey, Mom, please don't cry. The doctor said it's a mild concussion. I'm totally fine."

Holly scrambled to her feet and looked at her only son, who had woken up and was smiling at her.

Her heart soared. "Will!" She knelt down at his bedside and smoothed his hair away from his face. "I wasn't crying over you," she said, giving him a watery smile. "I was crying over me."

"Well, I like that. What kind of mom are you? I've got the IV and the beeping machines and a really bad headache, and you're not crying over me?"

"Nope," she said, kissing him on the forehead. "Because you're totally fine. The doctor said so, remember?"

Will gave a dramatic sigh. "Years from now when I write my memoirs this is going to be a major chapter."

Her smile turned into a grin. "Will it be as major as the chapter where your mother marries your high school coach?"

Will's eyes widened. "Maybe I'm hallucinating. I think you should repeat that last thing."

"You heard me." Her smile faded. "Or at least, you'll be able to have a chapter where your mother proposes to your high school coach. I'm not so sure he's going to say yes."

"You're such a dope."

"You know, Alex says the same thing. If I'm such a dope, why would he want to marry me?"

"Honestly, I have no idea. Maybe he thinks you're cute."

Holly ran a hand through her tangled hair. "Not right now, I'm not. I think I should wait a few days before I make my move. If my looks are all I have going for me…"

"Oh, no, you don't," Will said, looking stern. "Look, they're going to kick you out of my room before long, and, anyway I need to rest. I do have a concussion, you know."

"A mild concussion."

"Okay, fine. The next time I want a little sympathy I'll break both my legs. The point is, you could sit out there in the waiting room all night, or you could go to Alex's house and ask him to marry you, so we can wrap this thing up and move on to living happily ever after. I expect to see the two of you here at my bedside tomorrow morning, hand in hand. I've waited long enough, and so has Alex."

Holly raised one eyebrow. "Since when do you tell me what to do?"

"Since now. This is it, Mom. You've taught me everything I know about guts and courage and going after what you want. It's time to practice what you preach."

"All joking aside, Squirt, there's a chance Alex will turn me down."

"I suppose there is. Are you going to let that stop you?"

He was looking stern again, and Holly couldn't keep the smile off her face. "No, I'm not," she said, bending down to tuck the covers more closely around him and straightening up again. "Got any ideas on how I should propose?"

When she pulled up in Alex's driveway, the only light in his house came from his bedroom window. She slipped in through the front door as quietly as she could, turning on one small lamp and moving silently through the living room as she looked for the CD she wanted.

Before she played it, she gathered all the candles she could find and lit them, scattering them around and lighting a pathway from the living room to the stairs. She looked terrible, her jeans and Wildcats sweatshirt stained and a little damp, her hair wild and her eyes still red and swollen, but she couldn't help that. And, after all, Alex had seen her look even worse.

She took a deep breath. Okay, she was ready. She walked over to the stereo and hit the play button.

And then Marvin Gaye's voice was filling the house.

She stood in the middle of the living room and waited, and before long Alex was coming down the stairs, past all the candles she had lit, until he stood just a few feet away from her.

"What's going on?" he asked, his voice carefully neutral. He was wearing a pair of gray sweatpants, barefoot and bare chested, and it was so good to see him again she felt tears pricking behind her eyes.

She took a deep breath. "Will sent me here," she said, and then shook her head. "No, I mean, I wanted to come. I wanted to tell you—to tell you—" She paused, biting her lip, while he just looked at her.

Damn him, anyway. Why couldn't he back her up against a wall again? *Make* her say it? What if she didn't have the courage to say it on her own?

She took another breath. "What I mean to say—what I want to say—"

Alex folded his arms across his chest. "You're terrible at this."

"Shut up. What I want to say—what I mean to say— okay, you're right, I suck. Dammit, Alex, I—I love you. I want—that is—will you dance with me?" she asked, holding out her hand.

Alex was still for a moment. "That depends," he said finally, and Holly's hand dropped to her side. Alex took a step closer, and then another, until he was right in front of her. For a long minute they stood like that, and then Alex took both her hands in his. "Will you marry me, Holly?"

She took two quick steps backward. "What? No! I mean, I was supposed to ask you! I thought I'd ask you to dance first, you know, to sort of work up to it, but then you jumped the gun and—"

Alex was grinning now. "Will you marry me, Holly?"

She came close again, her eyes meeting his. "Yes," she said, and joy flooded through her, unadulterated by any doubt or fear. She knew Alex could see all that joy, burning through her like sunlight, and then he was kissing her and that burned too, and Holly wondered how she'd ever been able to walk away from this. At least that was one mistake she'd never make again.

"We have to tell Will," Alex said, when they could finally pull away from one another.

"Visiting hours are over. We can't see him till to-morrow morning."

Alex thought about it. "Want to make out in the hospital waiting room?"

For some reason that made Holly burst into tears. "Yes, I do," she managed to say, throwing her arms around Alex. "I really, really do."

And they did. They drove back to the hospital and sat down in the lobby, and they held hands, and they kissed, and they talked quietly until morning. Then they walked hand in hand into Will's hospital room, just like he'd wanted them to.

Epilogue

His wedding day.

Alex thought this should be a quietly serious moment, a moment to contemplate the future in some sort of deep and profound manner, but that wasn't an option when you had Will for a best man.

"Okay, Coach, I went online to get all the advice-to-the-bridegroom I could find. Number one—when you're standing at the altar, bend your knees slightly. Apparently if you hold them stiff it can cut off the circulation and make you pass out or something. Number two—"

"Will, in the name of everything holy, please stop talking. Why do they make us wait back here, anyway? I can't tell if they're ready."

Will looked sympathetic. "Starting to get nervous, huh? That's totally normal, by the way. One of my most important jobs is to keep you calm. Would you like me to tell you a joke? I know this really good—"

Alex took Will by the lapels of his tuxedo. "I just need two things. Tell me if I look okay, and tell me if they're ready for us out there."

Will stepped back and studied him appraisingly. Alex stood up straight and tried to look easy, confident and manly. In reality he felt a little sick, but he hoped that didn't show.

"Actually, you look a little sick. Do you want some Pepto Bismol? I brought some in my emergency best-man kit."

"You have an emergency best-man kit?" Alex asked, momentarily distracted.

"You bet. It's got—"

"No, don't tell me. Just sneak out front and see if they—"

Before he could finish the sentence the little door opened and the minister popped his head in. "Showtime!" he said cheerfully, and Alex wondered if he had a few minutes to go to the bathroom and throw up.

Will patted him on the back. "It's okay, Coach," he said. "We made it to the state championship and we're going to make it through this. Right?"

Alex managed to nod. He took a deep breath, and then he and Will went through the door to stand on the left side of the altar.

The church was full of people but Alex didn't see any of them very clearly. His eyes were fixed at the back of the church, where Holly would be appearing any minute. He remembered what Will had said and bent his knees slightly.

The music began. It was something by Bach, played

on the piano. It was probably very beautiful, but Alex wouldn't have noticed if it had been the theme to *Star Wars* or the Oscar Mayer wiener jingle.

He took a breath. Gina was coming down the aisle with the measured steps they'd practiced at the rehearsal yesterday. She was probably very beautiful, too, but she could have been hopping along in a pink gorilla suit and Alex wouldn't have noticed that, either.

There must have been some kind of musical cue, because all at once everyone in the church was rising to their feet. Alex felt his heart stop. He bent his knees a little more and took another deep breath.

And there she was.

As soon as he saw Holly all his fear melted away. Alex had lived thirty-five years, and in all that time no one had ever looked at him like this. There was so much love and trust and joy in Holly's face that she seemed to glow, as if she were lit from within.

He hadn't been allowed to see her dress until now. It was nothing like he'd expected, especially the full skirt, which was frilly and feminine and as impractical as a fairy tale…and so beautiful it made his throat ache. Through the mist of her veil he could see her smile, and the extra shimmer in her eyes that came from tears.

Before he knew what was happening he was crying too. He started to lift his arm to wipe away the tears with his sleeve, but then Will was handing him a handkerchief. "Emergency kit," he whispered.

"Thanks," Alex whispered back, and suddenly he was grinning at Will, and at Holly, and Holly was smiling at them both with all the love in her heart.

Then his soul mate was standing before him, putting her hands in his, and Holly and Alex were promising out loud and before God what they'd promised in their hearts long ago. And when they sealed their promise with a kiss, they knew that happily-ever-after had just begun.

* * * * *